THE HUNTSMAN OF CORVINUS

by

Timothy Bryan

THE HUNTSMAN OF CORVINUS

First published in the United States 2022
Printed in the United States of America

"Graveyards are the place of important and irreplaceable dreams . . .'Tis better to cherish the mundane moments of our present."

Contents

Chapter One

The inner city was lit by pale lights illuminating an extended stretch of concrete and brick buildings. Bars covered the lower-level windows facing a busy street, and light bloomed from behind opaque windows in squat apartment blocks.

It was fully night, and cars zoomed past these austere structures making up Budapest's Eighth district. Honking horns and squeaking brakes echoed from passing commuters as they drove home to more affluent suburbs.

The gritty streets they left behind were full of working girls, most of whom were beginning their own version of shift work in the urban environment.

Sprinkled throughout the rough area were occasional ambulance sirens, which resounded off age-old buildings as the emergency vehicles twisted through the constricted avenues of the dense central European metropolis.

This urban location was not a wealthy one. It consisted of dirty streets littered with discarded liquor bottles and vague heaps of assorted cardboard. The collected refuse of crowded tenements filled the air with a pungent stench as everyday garbage awaited pickup from rat-infested receptacles and graffiti-covered bins.

Dark shapes of numerous people ambled through the area as it closed down for the day. Urban retirees and blue-collar workers competed for space on sidewalks that offered dog excrement up to the unsuspecting shoes of plodding pedestrians.

At the intersection of a side street, dull light cascaded down from a public lamppost. To one side stood another broken lamp, so the illumination below was uneven, casting patchy shadows into the darkness of an alleyway. The barely lit side street extended back for fifty yards.

Down that alley were sets of more garbage cans and rusted bins, lined up for orderly collection in the squalid environment. Their placement made the sheltered space beyond the containers ideal for privacy in the dead-end alley, ensuring it was an oasis of calm tucked away from the prying eyes of the bustling city.

Gabor stood in that fading light of brick-lined back street. Of considerable height, he had once been a strapping man, but life on the streets had transformed him into a doddering, unhealthy vagrant. His tawdry clothes were stained with unnamable liquids, and holes in his frayed jacket revealed mismatched and layered clothing below. Beneath, hidden within his arrangement of disheveled apparel, were multitudes of pockets, stuffed with all manner of ketchup packets and seasoning supplies for future use.

On his worn and wrinkled face, Gabor wore a toothless grin. Patches of stubble grew across his ruddy cheeks, giving him a strangely merry appearance in the shifting light. Leering, he wiped away snot with a crusted half-glove as he considered his fortunes for the night.

Gabor looked down at his feet with an approving nod. Below him lay his pile of possessions, with various plastic bags holding personal items and stashes of booze. He had even managed to score a cache of expensive hand cream that someone from a local hotel had thrown away. All in all, they were the goods of someone who liked to travel light and self-medicate.

"Ha, I knew we would get it tonight," Gabor said, his mood growing ecstatic. "Sometimes, you just gotta get here early. It's never easy to get this spot. You just settle in after the cops come by. They clear out the competition and throw 'em in the shelters."

Raising his bloodshot eyes, Gabor glanced to the side and met Bianka's gaze. She was also well into midlife, and addiction issues and poor hygiene likewise marred her swaying physique. With a grimy complexion that complemented her filthy clothing, she clutched a cheap bottle of wine in her palsied fingers. Nodding vigorously, she surveyed the dirty, cold environment.

"Yeah, I'm not giving it up," said Bianka, focusing on Gabor with a confident and dreamy smile. "Just let someone try to take this spot from us."

Staggering toward the dead end of the alley, Bianka set down some ratty blankets in a semblance of order as she prepared for the night ahead. Still gripping the bottle, she scanned the worn walls encircling their precious sleeping spot.

Gabor nodded eagerly, his eyes catching in sudden remembrance of an important memory. Grunting, he dug into his pockets and pulled out a wad of cash. The brightly colored Hungarian banknotes were crumpled and smeared with dirt, as if they had been dipped in congealed soy sauce.

Counting carefully, he scrunched up several bills as he struggled to access distant mathematical skills in his frayed memory. Losing his place, he started over, trying again for an accurate appraisal of the money's value.

With a frustrated grimace, Gabor gave up entirely. Stuffing the soiled cash back into his pocket, he lowered his voice into a conspiratorial whisper. "I told ya, the best way to get donations is to hound the weak ones. . .and the women. They always give something when they don't wanna deal with us. It's just a matter of them understandin' that we deserve something. They got to pay the less fortunate."

Bianka smiled at Gabor through her alcohol-dulled senses.

"You always right, Gabor," Bianka replied, holding up her bottle and trying to read the ingredients in the fuzzy light. "Nobody is smarter than you in the whole city. Don't know what I'd do...without you."

Gabor beamed with modest appreciation of himself, playing the role of reluctant genius as he considered their fortunate location in this highly prized alleyway. He surveyed his surroundings like a conquering general, making sure everything was in the right place for a night of relaxed drinking and mind-numbing intoxication.

After a moment, Gabor became confused. Fiddling in his pockets, he searched for something. After the effort proved fruitless, he shrugged and leaned down to his belongings.

Pulling out a rumpled pack of cigarettes from a bag, he withdrew a bent one and expertly popped it into the corner of his mouth. After digging out a book of matches, he struggled and managed to light it on only the third try.

Leaning back, he inhaled deeply, forcing the precious smoke into his abused lungs. Grimacing, he fought the urge to cough as the toxins flooded his bloodstream. Rubbing his whiskers, he uttered a contented sigh and settled into a standing stupor.

At the entrance of the alley, from the point where it met the street, Gabor noticed something strange. The Huntsman stood in the half-light, staring down the alley toward them. Tall, even more so than Gabor, he remained still and silent as he watched the homeless couple.

Gabor squinted down at the alley's entrance, trying to make out the odd observer. Raising his voice, his face flushed with anger. "Hey, we're sleeping here tonight. We got it first, so get outta here."

The darkness continued to hide their visitor, and the figure offered no response to Gabor's claim of ownership. The silhouetted Huntsman remained unmoving, his silence making Gabor more uneasy with every passing second.

Scowling, Gabor thought for a moment. Tossing aside his cigarette, he grabbed an empty bottle from the ground. Striding to the alley wall, he smashed it against the cold stone surface.

Holding up the improvised weapon, Gabor raised his voice higher, motioning to the stranger with the jagged glass shiv. "We don't want any trouble, but we'll give you plenty if ya fuck with us. You don't wanna find out the hard way. We ain't playing with ya."

Such a threat was not idle. Gabor had ended many fights in his life using his size and weight to devastating effect. Anyone who mattered on the streets knew better than to cross him, and this fucker would be sorry if he tried pushing them around.

But in response the observer remained silent, even as his head tilted perceptibly toward Gabor. Apparently unworried, the stranger's face was hidden beneath the shadow of a strange hood, offering no hint of identity or intention.

Becoming animated, Bianka gestured toward the dark figure, her voice uneasy. "Gabor, maybe we should give it up. I don't like the look of that guy."

Stopping, then hesitantly shaking his head, Gabor stepped toward the alley's entrance and their quiet observer.

"I said, we..." Gabor began, but his voice faded as unease crept across his features.

Up close, Gabor saw that the Huntsman was massive. His cloth hood still concealed his face, but a thick white beard spilled from under that odd-looking cowl. His build was solid, and his clothing looked strange, almost theatrical, as if he had stepped out of an ancient play.

Disturbed, Gabor saw that he looked nothing like a fellow street dweller.

Gabor stopped, unsure of how or whether to proceed. Shaking his head, he dropped the bottle and turned back toward Bianka.

Shuffling back, he motioned to the collection of their possessions on the ground. His jerky movements were hurried, his voice tight with fear. "Get our stuff together. To hell with this."

As he came closer to Bianka, the sound of scraping footsteps echoed behind Gabor. His eyes widened, and panic crept into face as he frantically gestured toward their belongings.

Bianka didn't seem to understand. Her intoxicated gaze met his as she smacked her lips, preparing to take another pull on her bottle.

A heavy impact struck Gabor from behind, hurling him toward Bianka. With a vicious thud, he plowed into his unaware companion, and they crashed into filthy wall behind her.

Suddenly, he was staring down at her from only inches away. A long, dark shaft protruded from his abdomen, and his eyes darted about, struggling to grasp this strange new situation.

The weapon continued onward, having also pierced Bianka. They were held up and pinned together by the long spear, with its sharp tip embedded deep into the brick behind them. The weapon's shaft was black as night, its entire length consisting of a dark obsidian-like substance.

Jerking weakly against the shaft, the skewered Gabor looked down at Bianka. Working her jaw, she coughed violently, blood escaping in gouts from her convulsing lips.

She tried to respond to what was happening, but only strained gurgles came from her quivering mouth. Confused, broken sounds emerged from her throat, and terrified alarm altered her weathered expression as she tried to grasp her suddenly grave condition.

Gabor's gaze dropped again, disbelief overtaking his mind as blood splashed beneath them. It felt unreal, as though he were watching something detached from himself, like a nightmare unfolding at a distance. Much like a hideous snuff film, he found himself at the center of a scene he didn't think possible.

Peering back at Bianka, he saw that her eyes had already drifted elsewhere, and she was no longer anchored to the physical world.

Behind him, the sound of striding feet grew closer. A dark hand seized his head and wrenched it back, exposing Gabor's pale neck. An equally black knife, of the same substance as the spear before, began to saw through his flesh, swiftly flaying the skin open and cutting into the vessels and arteries underneath.

Gushing blood cascaded from the injury as Gabor vainly grabbed at both the weapon and the spurting wound.

With a savage twist of his grip, the attacker wrenched the head free from the flailing body, and Gabor's headless corpse collapsed against his deceased girlfriend in the shadows of the alleyway.

* * *

The sun shone down on a mass of people and vehicles moving across the extensive city landscape. Tides of bodies jostled for space among buses, cars, and sidewalks beneath the cloudless sky of central Budapest.

Nearby, crowds poured out of the underground metro, colliding and separating as commuters moved in opposing directions. The dull roar of cars and beeping horns was matched by the raised voices of pedestrians going about their hectic daily schedule.

Around a central gathering point for buses and transferring workers, a series of advertising signs flickered atop buildings, parking garages, and a nearby mall. Some of the signs announced international brands, while others advertised office space or the names of specific businesses.

The controlled turmoil of the central square throbbed with people, like a living arterial delivery system for the city's functioning body.

Through the busy streets, a tram trundled past crowds of students and workers. Intent on reaching their morning destinations, few in the bustling population paid attention to their nearby environments. Instead, they went about their mornings, and the predominant interaction between neighbors was the universal habit of scrolling on mobile phones, texting, and checking social media.

To the side of the thronging commuters sat a few elderly pensioners, along with occasional clusters of the homeless. Perched on scattered benches, both groups watched the morning travel with interest, but for entirely different reasons. The former group hoped wistfully for a time long past, while the latter longed for a different outcome in the present. In either circumstance, the mainstream commuters ignored them as they hurried through their busy lives.

Inside a clattering tram, Monica Varga stood with one hand clasped around a grab handle as the vehicle wound through cramped avenues of the bustling city. The blond twelve-year-old had sharp eyes and a precocious manner as she observed her fellow morning travelers. Dressed in a private school uniform, she stood out among the working-class riders of public transportation.

Bored, Monica let her gaze wander around the car, searching for something to occupy her interest. Focusing ahead, her eyes came to rest on the back of a shiny skull. The clean-shaven head belonged to a young woman standing directly in front of her, and on the back of her smooth scalp was a bizarre tattoo of a vicious-looking Viking with numerous bright flowers woven through its ragged beard.

The strange and colorful body art represented a cross between a bloodthirsty conqueror and a pacifistic flower child.

Monica stared at the woman for some time, contorting her features in a confused frown at the odd but intriguing artistry.

The young woman abruptly turned around, noticing Monica and glaring down at her in disapproval. Clearly unamused by the child's attention, she lifted her lip in annoyance.

To the side, Monica's mother tugged at her daughter's arm in a plea for manners. In her mid-thirties, Erica Varga's frown lines had not yet ruined her good looks, but her strained features still suggested a woman unhappy with the course of her life.

Despite her dour demeanor, Erica's dark, shoulder-length hair remained free of gray, and she still maintained an attractive figure, one still capable of holding its own against gravity.

Erica offered the tattooed woman an apology in the form of a nod and a bashful smile. She was not exactly ashamed of Monica, but her daughter's behavior often forced her to smooth things over in the interest of politeness.

Erica smiled to herself, realizing she was hardly the only parent accustomed to such gestures. In fact, she mused that it had become something of a pastime for many parents in today's spoiled-child world to soothe the hurt feelings of strangers because of rude kids who never felt the need to show respect.

Monica relented and shifted her gaze away from the tattooed girl. Smirking at her mother, she scanned the car for other interesting people to watch. Nothing in the immediate area caught her attention, and her eyes drifted to the window, through which she could see hordes of intriguing possibilities hustling through the crowded streets. Life was always full of interesting sights for those willing to look, and Monica was always willing.

Frowning, Erica turned away from her daughter and stared out her own window with practiced detachment. She felt somber, her eyes jumping from one city landmark to another as the clanking vehicle lurched along the busy road.

When the tram finally came to a stop, mother and daughter waited to exit last to avoid the surge of me-first humanity moving to depart. When their turn finally came, Erica motioned for Monica to step off first in a quiet show of parental humility.

Monica smiled her thanks and stepped into the daylight, followed by her hurried mother. As they waded into the river of people, they were quickly swallowed by the surging crowd.

* * *

Much of the morning commute had wound down. Computer, phone, and souvenir shops along Hunyadi János Street displayed consumer goods from their windows but for now remained empty as the businesses waited for their first customers of the day. Bored shopkeepers stood beside their storefronts, looking disappointed and expectant.

Monica walked ahead of her mother, skipping across the cracked concrete of a disused sidewalk. She smiled back at Erica, showing off considerable agility as she pivoted and extended one leg in a mock-ballet pose.

Gathering herself, Monica performed a serviceable pirouette on the stained concrete, even managing to finish in the correct direction—toward her mom.

"Mom, why didn't you ever take ballet classes?" Monica asked. "It'd be nice to practice with someone outside of lessons."

Toting a heavy bag of books and struggling to keep pace with her carefree daughter, Erica wasn't amused. Frowning, she kept her voice level. "Not everyone got to grow up in the Castle District and take private lessons, Mon. Or had parents who took turns spoiling her."

At the mention of competing parents, Monica's playful look melted away. Frowning, she fell into step beside her mom, adopting the monotonous walk of a gloomy urban pedestrian as she peered at the empty sidewalk.

Feeling guilty for being cross, Erica changed the subject and tried to sound more upbeat. "You've got that math test today, right? You ready for it?"

"Mom, I hate math. Why do I have to learn this stuff, anyhow?" Monica asked. "You don't even remember half of it, and you're a college professor. I gotta take my math homework to Dad most of the time."

Erica frowned at the comment but also nodded at its truth. She couldn't blame her daughter for being honest—*and* right.

"I teach English literature. Calculus isn't exactly a requirement for my job. Besides, your dad works in insurance, so he needs those skills. Numbers were always his thing."

Monica glanced at her mother with a skeptical eye roll, making her opinion of the explanation clear.

"Yeah, so you get my point," Monica replied. "It's, like, totally useless to learn math unless I wanna work with it when I'm old like you."

The age remark did nothing to improve Erica's mood. She looked ahead to a massive stone building, where several children were already entering through the front doors. Frowning, she felt relieved at not having to defend her math skills. Discussions of her advancing age were also best to ignore.

"Just try to get along in your classes, dear," Erica said. "Life is full of things you don't like to do, but you still have to anyway. It sucks, but it's not going to change anytime soon."

Erica and Monica moved near the front entrance of her impressive school. Erica stopped and motioned to the open door. "Besides, you got pretty good grades in math. Maybe you can grow up to be a math professor?"

Monica wrinkled her nose at the idea. Glancing around, her eyes wandered, searching for more exciting spectacles to occupy her time.

Standing at the entrance, Monica's teacher, Andreas Horvath, waved at them. Middle-aged and paunchy, he smiled at Erica, holding his gaze on her for perhaps too long.

Monica noticed the extended stare. "Mom, Mr. Horvath is creepy. Now you know why I hate math. And his wife is even worse. She measures our skirts to make sure they fit right. Says she has to make sure we're dressed properly, or we get sent home."

Erica frowned as she tried to decipher the complex situation her daughter was describing. "Well, you're always properly dressed, so no worries. Anyway, it's your last day of school, so try to make it a good one..."

Erica trailed off as she noticed Monica was ignoring her and making eye contact with friends as they trickled in from the street. Monica smiled eagerly at each familiar face, waiting to be set free from parental prison.

"And don't let your father get you any of that Chinese food when he picks you up. I have healthy food at home," Erica added.

Monica's face contorted in disgust. "Mom, that food is gross. Hanna says they use cat meat in it."

Erica shook her head and patted Monica on the shoulder, trying to sound confident.

"Mon, they don't put cat meat in it," Erica said, though she didn't appear entirely certain herself.

Not responding, Monica looked toward the road where her classmate Hanna hurried toward her with a big grin. Erica smiled down at Monica's best friend, then waved to Hanna's mother in the BMW that just dropped her off.

When Erica looked back, her daughter was already entering the school at Hanna's side. Gone without even a cursory goodbye, Erica felt a pang of disappointment and grimaced. "Bye, Mon. Love you too. Have a good day."

Sighing, Erica adjusted the book bag on her shoulder and walked away from the crowds of arriving children.

* * *

Erica sat at her desk, a large and cheap one made of pressed board and glue. Stacked around her was a collection of folders, all bursting with reports and theses of various sizes. The sheer volume of papers gave the impression that the desk might buckle under their weight. A laptop sat in the center, shiny and unopened for the moment.

Around her, the office was small but pleasant. A photo of John Wayne hung on the wall, and the Duke looked down on her with that captivating grin, the one that said *I am the coolest man alive, and we both know it.*

Wearing her too-large reading glasses, Erica held an ink gel pen in her hand and clicked it several times, trying to get it to function. The paper beneath it was heavily marked, but caught in a battle with the malfunctioning pen, she was unable to continue her corrections.

Frustrated, she rifled through the desk in search of another pen. With a celebratory grunt, she pulled another from a drawer, raising it overhead like it was the Olympic torch on its final leg.

A gentle tap on her open office door distracted Erica from her victory. Evi stood in the doorway, looking at Erica as though she had lost her mind. In her forties, attractive and bright-eyed, Evi wore the smile of someone who always knew what you were thinking, even if you had never met.

"How was class? Did you see that Bulgarian guy?" Evi asked, her grin stretching impossibly wide. "He's not too young, and I hear he's available. Ripe for the plundering."

Erica frowned, a slight blush coloring her cheeks. "I saw him, but I also pay attention to my work contract. Especially that part about not dating our students. You may have heard of it. You know, in that large stack of papers you signed?"

The grin melted from Evi's face as she shrugged with feigned innocence. "You ever notice how people in charge never follow their own rules? I mean, when I worked at the U of A, we had a tenured physicist who slept with every young assistant in his department.

Everybody knew it, but nobody did anything. He just kept on keepin' on, if you know what I mean."

Flicking the new pen, Erica struggled to make it write. After scraping the paper without leaving a mark, she gave up and tossed it across the room, where it clanked off a garbage can and fell to the floor. Erica frowned at her poor aim.

"Why didn't you do something about it?" Erica asked, clearly uninterested in a real answer. "You had a responsibility to protect the integrity of the academic contract. All those young women relied on you to protect them."

"I would've, but I was sleeping with him too," Evi replied, unbothered by guilt. "And it's never easy to find a quality hookup. You wouldn't believe what he could do with his—"

"What brings you here, Evi?" Erica cut in. "Don't you have a class soon?"

Evi scowled, discouraged by the interruption. "I did, but they canceled it. They said it was because some student had typhus or something. Said he could infect us all."

Erica rolled her eyes and peered up at her. "Typhus? In Hungary?"

"I'm not a doctor. That's not my specialty," Evi responded, shrugging. "I just follow the rules as they're presented to me. If they want to cancel my class, who am I to argue?"

Evi raised her eyes. Her gaze drifted to the John Wayne poster. Thoughtful, she concentrated, as if contemplating some great existential issue.

Stepping closer to Erica's desk, Evi changed the subject. "Did you check out that app?"

Erica removed her reading glasses, trying to appear surprised at the question. "Yeah, I tried it. And...I got a date."

Evi's face lit up as she reached out for a high-five. Erica lightly tapped her fingers, clearly not enthusiastic.

"It feels weird being on the market again," Erica admitted, sounding embarrassed. "I feel like a piece of meat. I forgot what it's like to be available."

Nodding knowingly, Evi grinned and pulled out her phone. Swiping across several screens, she held it in front of Erica.

"How's that for meat?" Evi asked, leering perversely.

Erica glanced at the screen, then quickly turned away. Fighting a grin, she shook her head. "You're a sick woman. Why would you show me that? You're like a schoolgirl, except middle-aged and less mature. In fact, you make Madonna look like a retired nun."

Evi chuckled and slipped the phone back into her pocket. Smiling, she leaned near Erica, adopting a wise tone—the voice of a sage. "Being single, especially after two years, means you can sample all the meat you want. You need some meat in your life. We all do."

Erica leaned back in her chair, visibly uncomfortable. Sighing, she met her friend's outlandish grin. "Dick pics and daily encounters aren't for all of us, Evi. I need something more than that."

Evi shrugged and straightened herself, planting her hands on her waist in a display of promiscuous pride. Abruptly, she turned and headed for the door.

Glancing back, she offered a suggestive smile. "That's what I used to say, until I learned how to have fun."

With nothing further to add, Evi strolled from the office, bouncing and swaying her hips in an exaggerated motion.

Watching her go, Erica shook her head and chuckled at the spectacle. Turning back to her papers and cluttered desk, she began anew her search for a functioning pen.

Chapter Two

The afternoon traffic meandered between tall office buildings and jumbled crowds. The beeping of horns from aggressive cars was matched by slow buses and timed stoplights, as if the entire traffic enterprise was working to infuriate restless drivers on the cramped streets.

Groups of pedestrians stood patiently on the sidewalks, awaiting their chance to cross at intersections last painted when communism was the law of the land. None of the indifferent faces appeared concerned by the chaotic swarms of vehicles zooming along the undersized streets in front of them.

Laszlo Varga was one of those untamed, irritable drivers, and he gesticulated wildly as he banged on his steering wheel. With a drooping seventies mustache and excessive hair gel, he looked like an impatient porn-star cabbie, even if his dark Saab didn't fit the profile of a taxi. Though in his early forties, the last four decades of fashion sense seemed to have passed him by.

Laszlo checked his mirrors with manic eyes and stomped on the gas. Frustrated, he weaved around a garbage truck and accelerated toward a yellow light, one that turned red long before the car cleared the intersection.

To his side, Monica frowned with a combination of disappointment and practiced reservation. Such an expression was clearly one she was accustomed to. "Dad, why are we rushing? You just saved, like, thirty seconds."

Keeping his eyes roaming, Laszlo smiled from the corner of his mouth. "I have an appointment to keep, and these crappy drivers are gonna make me late. It's like they're trying to piss me off. Nobody knows how to drive here."

Monica stared over at Laszlo, pursing her lips and adopting a disapproving glare. "Dad, don't talk like that."

Sneaking a glance her way, a genuine smile crossed Laszlo's apologetic features. Extending his arm, he tousled her hair with obvious affection. "Sorry, sweetie."

Gesturing toward the plastic bags at her feet, Laszlo grinned. The containers of Chinese food were hardly touched, but he was excited as he considered the indeterminate delicacies. "Did you like the food? They always got a special. I can't imagine why everyone doesn't eat there."

Monica curled her lip, making her opinion of Laszlo's culinary choices clear. "Not really. Mom's just going to throw them away, just like last time."

Laszlo shrugged, refusing to let his daughter's dislike of the food dissuade him from buying it—again.

As he continued his rapid drive, Laszlo's dreamy eyes drifted toward a woman in her early twenties, dressed in a tight skirt at the side of the road. For once, he slowed as he passed her, craning his neck while the young woman ignored him.

The car continued rolling, drifting through a red light as Laszlo's gaze followed the skirted woman in the rearview mirror. Embarrassed, Monica covered her face with her hands.

Returning to his senses, Laszlo realized his mistake. He made a show of focusing straight ahead as Monica kept her face hidden.

"Sweetie, what is it?" Laszlo asked. "The light was gonna turn green anyway. I was just—"

Flashing lights lit up the car, and Laszlo rolled his eyes at the injustice of the police's sudden attention. "Oh shit, not again."

Laszlo eased the car to the curb near a busy restaurant. Sighing, he tugged at his mustache, a nervous habit which made him appear sleazy.

Nearby, a cluster of curious diners near the sidewalk perked up from their conversations and watched the unfolding ticket drama. Amused expressions and empathetic faces followed the policeman as he exited his car and approached Laszlo's vehicle from behind.

"I sure miss the days when you could just tip them and avoid a real fine," said Laszlo. "Life was so much better. Except for the occasional arrest, you could really be yourself."

When the police officer approached the window, Laszlo meekly handed over his driver's license and insurance papers.

Monica peeked from behind her hands as the unseen officer brusquely snatched the documents from Laszlo's grip. As he paced away, his shadow slid across the tinted side window while he returned to his patrol car.

Staring at the policeman for a moment, Monica shifted her gaze out her own window. Two baggy-clothed teenage boys stood on the sidewalk, each holding a half-eaten sandwich. The young men, skinny and annoying, snickered with smug expressions as they pointed at the traffic stop.

Monica frowned and looked away, avoiding the leering adolescents.

* * *

With a gloomy expression, Monica waved as her dad's car sped away. Gaining speed, Laszlo swerved around a cluster of tightly clad bicyclists as he disappeared down the twisting streets, leaving the fitness enthusiasts behind to shake their heads at his reckless driving.

Around Monica, the Castle District buzzed with noise and motion. The area was packed with tourists taking in the sights of the ancient neighborhood. Their raised eyes studied the surrounding buildings as they shuffled across weathered cobblestones and discolored pavement.

The district was dotted with stout apartment buildings and historical landmarks. Concrete blocks and brick construction mixed with peeling mortar, lending a medieval ambiance to the touristy area. Studded with structures that had seen both war and peace on an elongated timescale, the busy location appeared as something of a mecca for architectural buffs.

At street level, shops facing the pedestrian-only walkways were filled with enthusiastic travelers. Grinning shoppers clutched photos and expensive knickknacks depicting various sites throughout the capital region. Often missed by these buyers were the small inscriptions reading *Made in Indonesia* or other countries, tucked away on hidden points beneath their recent purchases.

In small grocery stores that catered to locals, people stepped into the bright day with their arms full of groceries. Heading back to their residences, the inhabitants ignored the throngs of visitors packing the many nearby cafés and restaurants.

It was a bustling and attractive environment.

Preoccupied, Monica focused on her feet as she angled through the crowds of strangers. Carrying her dad's gourmet takeout in a plastic bag, her thoughts drifted inward. As she stumbled along, her detached gaze stopped taking in the sights and sounds around her.

As Monica neared her apartment block, her schoolbag weighed heavily on her shoulders in the afternoon heat. Her glazed expression became aimless and flushed as her legs worked in a steady patter across the sun-warmed stones of the square.

A tap on her shoulder startled her, and she turned to see her friend Hanna. Leaning in to hug her, Hanna had an unreserved smile and an eager expression.

Returning the embrace, Monica smiled and brushed a wisp of hair from her squinting eyes.

"I missed you at the end of school," Hanna said, looking disappointed. "Connor said you went home early."

"Yeah," Monica replied. "My dad came early to get me again. He's not very patient when it's his turn to pick me up. Makes it hard to know when I'm going home."

Hanna shook her head, unconcerned. "Doesn't matter. But you missed Attila getting in a fight with that kid from Serbia. Mr. Horvath had to break them up. I didn't even know he could walk up a flight of stairs, let alone grab two kids by the collars and haul them away. And...who would've thought an international school would have a fistfight on the last day? I thought it cost too much for that kind of thing. It was kind of ghetto."

Monica smiled at her friend but said nothing.

Sighing, Hanna changed the subject. "Are you going to the zoo tomorrow? Mom says it's optional since school is officially over."

Monica nodded, motioning toward her apartment building. "Yeah, it'll be more exciting than watching TV alone. Besides, that'll be our last field trip as sixth graders. I'm going to miss our classroom."

With a forlorn expression, Monica gestured ahead to her building. Stepping deliberately, she moved with some reservation, like she had forgotten something and was unsure if she should continue. Hanna, unworried, fell into step beside her and matched her pace.

Moving in the opposite direction, colorful groups of mixed-age tourists passed them, chattering in a barrage of foreign languages as they pointed at varied historical monuments. Still moving carefully, Monica stepped aside, smiling as she gave them room to pass.

To the side of their intended path stood a large stone fountain. Depicting historical figures frozen in strange poses, it drew clusters of tourists. Standing nearby, a tour guide stood at the center of the crowd, motioning for everyone to gather closer.

As they continued, Monica drifted nearer to the gaggle of tourists. Coming to a stop, she put her hand across her chest, as if testing for her heartbeat by touch. Overwhelmed, her eyes slipped into a light trance as the tour guide's cadenced voice became clearer.

"...represents one of the finest examples of neobaroque sculpture," proclaimed the plump tour guide, a bespectacled man in his fifties. "The fountains even managed to avoid damage in the Second World War and demonstrate the mastery—"

Snapping her fingers in front of Monica's face, Hanna leaned closer and tried getting her attention. "Monica? Come back to Earth."

Startled from her daydream, Monica smiled bashfully. Turning her head, she took in the area like she was seeing it for the first time.

"Sorry…just felt dizzy," Monica said, blinking several times. "I'm just a little woozy. Must've been out in the sun too long."

Hanna waved her off, grinning as she glanced at the crowd near the fountain. "If I had to listen to that every day, I'd get dizzy too."

Catching herself, Monica's gaze steadied. Coming fully to her senses, she smiled brightly, and she hugged Hanna in a pleasant goodbye.

Waving energetically, Hanna skipped off into the throngs of tourists, bouncing with each step as she hopscotched through the milling strangers.

While Hanna moved away, Monica watched her go. Staring into the crowd, she tried to pinpoint what had unsettled her. Something had been off, like the world had shifted for a few seconds. *Weird.*

After taking a moment, she finally shrugged it off, and turning, she bounded toward her building with renewed energy.

Monica's home was in a large, clean set of apartments housed behind an old nineteenth-century façade off the main square. The lobby area of the imposing building was luxurious, with a receptionist seated behind a broad desk inside the glass front entrance.

As Monica opened the entrance door, she made eye contact with a uniformed security woman behind the desk, who had a surprisingly pleasant demeanor on her face, something that was unusual for Hungarian employees. The chubby woman seemed to really enjoy her job, which was even more surprising for the sometimes-depressing culture of the capital city.

Smiling, Monica returned the guard's cheerful mood and walked toward the bank of elevators along the lobby's back wall. Pressing the button to go up, she looked sourly down at the plastic bag she carried, then leaned over and dropped the dreaded Chinese food into a nearby trash receptacle.

* * *

Outside, darkness crept across the skyline, blotting out the last traces of remaining daylight. The fading sun left behind a strange beige glow that mingled with the remnants of fluffy clouds.

The apartment itself held undeniable appeal for any urban resident. It was clean and well-positioned, with multiple windows providing an unobstructed view of the tourist district below.

Perched above the Castle District, the residence commanded a pristine view of the soaring Matthias Church and the surrounding ancient walls. Because the district itself sat atop a hill above the rest of Budapest, visibility extended over the capital in every direction.

In ancient times, such a view would have been of immense military value. Owing to this historical significance, the apartment's centrality and prominence were unmatched elsewhere in the city. Kings and royalty had enjoyed this same view for more than a thousand years.

From the living room, the outward perspective stretched to encompass the Danube River, which separated opposite sides of the city. Buda lay to the west of the waterway, while Pest was on the east. Tourist boats and barges crisscrossed the powerful current that divided the city, making it appear haphazard and disorganized.

From such a commanding height, much of the higher Buda side was visible, with lines of car headlights marking various winding roads below. Across the river, the buildings of Pest glowed with their own brilliant lights, almost as if the two halves of the city were dueling in a silent contest for urban beauty across the venerable waterway.

Inside, the living space was filled with wooden furniture and tasteful decor. The kitchen and living rooms were part of an open-concept design, allowing someone to cook while still interacting with guests or family.

In the living room, three photo prints were spaced evenly on the high wall above the television. The first was Sammy Davis Jr., the middle was FDR, and the third showed Ronald Reagan. Somehow, despite the varied historical figures in each frame, the images were symmetrical with the mood and decor.

On the wall-mounted television, images of the murdered homeless people played, flashing between photos of the couple while they were alive and police numbers requesting tips regarding their deaths.

After a moment, the view switched to a camera focusing on the dirty alley where they had been murdered. In that grim area, numerous policemen examined the ground and walls with precision, running testing swabs across the concrete and brick surfaces.

Yellow police tape blocked off the alley from closer inspection, and a small crowd stood behind it, watching the officers work. The televised images were sad and worrisome for the capital city, as evidenced by the histrionic tone of the constantly updating news channel.

Erica watched the news program from a soft white couch. Worry lined her face, as if something nagged at the edges of her mind. Chewing her lip, she stared at the screen, becoming increasingly distressed while wrestling with an almost-realized memory.

Stewing in her thoughts, it took some time before she finally let go of her unease. Snapping back to the present, she breathed deep and tried to relax.

Peering down at her phone, the stress melted from her features as her attention shifted to the bright screen.

Getting happier, Erica's expression softened as she tapped on the keys. Eventually, the worry left her face entirely, and she grew more interested as the text conversation progressed.

Behind her, Monica emerged slowly from the hallway. Curious, she focused on her mother's back, remaining silent as she stepped closer. Intrigued, she peered over Erica's shoulder, carefully watching the activity on her phone.

"Mom, what are you doing?" Monica asked, furrowing her brow. "Who are you texting?"

Startled, Erica stood and nearly stumbled away from the couch. Flustered, she glanced around the apartment while slipping the phone into her pocket. Trying to appear calm and in control, she failed at both.

"Monica, um...nobody. I was just—" Erica muttered.

"Who's Adam?" Monica asked, her inquisitive stare sharpening into accusation.

Erica rubbed her hands together, searching for the right words—or at least a good convincing lie. Her voice turned evasive as she avoided Monica's stare.

"He's...just a friend," Erica explained, lying badly. "A lecturer at the social science department."

Monica regarded her mother skeptically, weighing the truth of Erica's statement. Silence settled between them as their eyes studied one another.

Fortuitously, Erica's phone rang in her pocket, and she quickly pulled it out, sighing with relief when she saw *Laszlo* on the screen. Monica's looming interrogation was momentarily interrupted.

"Hello, Laszlo," Erica said, putting her hand over her other ear to hear better.

After a moment, Erica's demeanor grew sour, and she bit her lip. "Yes, you said you would...what does that mean?"

She glanced up as she listened to Laszlo's words, keeping her tone low and avoiding her daughter's increasingly intense stare.

"Other people have lives too," Erica continued, frustration filling her voice. "Well, okay, but maybe next time you could give us a little more notice?"

Lowering the phone, Erica's unsettled gaze met Monica's. Hesitating, she frowned and pursed her lips.

Monica raised her eyebrows. "What did Dad say?"

Taking a breath, Erica shook her head in practiced disappointment. Gesturing toward the window, she spoke cooly. "Your father can't take you to the zoo tomorrow. He said he has meetings all day."

Monica's expression, already brooding, turned cold. She stared ahead, her eyes fixed and unblinking.

Taken aback, Erica stuttered. "It's...okay, Mon. I'll take you. I'll miss work...again."

Taking several deep breaths, Monica didn't respond. Shaking her head, she turned and paced down the hallway, ending the exchange and clicking her bedroom door shut.

Frowning, Erics returned her gaze to the TV, where coverage of the homeless murders continued unabated.

* * *

Outside, the sign above the Italian restaurant simply read *Ristorante*. It was a cozy and small place, and pedestrians struggled to avoid chairs lining the table-packed sidewalk running the length of its front. Loud chatter and animated expressions marked it as a popular, if not peaceful, place.

Inside, the sounds of social feasting were amplified by the tight confines of the crowded dining area. Large families, gorging on pasta, pizza, and breadsticks, filled the area.

Across the interior, hands extended wine glasses that clinked together from a half-dozen separate toasts, making for a merry atmosphere.

The main dining room housed too many chairs for too little space, and the resulting body heat produced flushed faces and sweaty brows. The roar of conversation made the restaurant as loud as a raucous sporting event.

Waiters scurried among the small sea of patrons, holding trays of food above their heads with admirable dexterity. Somewhere in the background, children took turns screaming, as if they were testing the threshold where permanent hearing damage would occur.

Tucked into the far back corner of the place was a simple table, barely large enough for two. Laszlo sat on one side of it, his face focused intensely across the cramped space.

Even in the uneven candlelight, the truth of his situation was obvious: he was smitten. His eyes lingered, and he made no attempt to curb his attraction. Running his fingers through his greasy hair, he smiled dreamily into the flickering glow.

Across the table sat Natalia, who was decidedly less enchanted with her date. In her thirties, Slavic, and stunning, she wore an expression that screamed, *You really think you can afford me?*

Natalia spoke in a controlled voice, her Russian accent crisp and eloquent. "I told you, I had to meet some clients later. I can't control such things."

Laszlo kept his puppy-dog eyes, holding his hands up in mock acceptance. "No problem, Natalia. I sell insurance for a living. Clients and meetings are a way of life. We all have to pay the bills."

Natalia grimaced. "Then why are you 'busting my balls,' as they say?"

Laszlo lowered his eyes. "The only problem is, I had to miss taking my daughter..."

Irritated, Natalia frowned. "She will have to live with it. You drive her around all week when her mother could do it. Why you do all the work? Is there a reason she has a daughter, or do Americans make habit of having men act as mothers?"

Steeling his jaw, Laszlo lost some of the overt affection he had been displaying. "She's a good kid. She's been through a lot..."

Suddenly, Natalia stood up. Straightening her too-tight skirt, she motioned to the back of the restaurant and flashed a contemptuous scowl. "I'll be right back. I need to go to the ladies' room."

Laszlo sighed as she angled toward the toilets in the back of the restaurant. Though decidedly less happy, he watched her attractive figure the entire way.

As she disappeared into the shadowy restroom area, Laszlo noticed an old lady giving him a dirty look. Glancing between Natalia and Laszlo, it was clear what she thought of him and his date. Embarrassed and suddenly out of his element, Laszlo peered down at his untouched soup.

* * *

Daylight had left the city, and the dark skyline stretched in all directions along the inner avenues of Budapest's main streets. The buildings throughout the center were rarely more than six stories high, so much of the sky was visible from street level.

Light leaked from the windows of never-ending office buildings along the main thoroughfare, providing a cozy backdrop above the dim glow of streetlamps. Apartment buildings ran behind the corporate structures, leading to neighborhoods more removed from the main streets. Crowded and pressed together, these older buildings had a timeless and comfortable feel, with pedestrians meandering around them on cracked and stained sidewalks.

Laszlo drove in a controlled manner along a narrow interior street. With a smile on his face, he no longer cared about the intricacies of too-slow vehicles and crowded avenues filled with hurried people.

Stopping at a red light, Laszlo patiently motioned to an old lady who needed extra time to cross the street. Smiling, he waved as she ambled in front of his idling car, with each step aided by a cane and a grimace of pain.

Looking down at his mobile, Laszlo grinned. Addressed to *Natalia,* he tapped out a quick message.

"Thanks for the date. I had a great time."

A honk from an impatient taxi behind him prompted Laszlo to proceed. With an apologetic wave and a carefree smile, he drove on under the now-green light.

Weaving gently through narrow streets, he squeezed past cars half parked on red-and-yellow-curbed sidewalks. Taking his time, he eased through the scant traffic until his headlights illuminated a sturdy and attractive building.

New and well-maintained, the structure announced its purpose with the glowing sign *Danube Pearl* indicating its exclusive apartment design and location.

The structure had a modern appearance, and its exterior walls were free from wear or graffiti. At its main entrance, a bored doorman stood silently, nodding at the occasional passersby.

Laszlo pointed his car along the side and drove down the street that bordered the elegant building. Turning into a garage entry, he pressed a red button and waited as the red entrance arm rose.

Staring wistfully, he adopted a detached and contented expression. Running a hand along his whiskered jaw, he bathed in the glow that could only accompany romantic success. *Life is good.*

Pulling inside, Laszlo took several turns in the tight-fitting basement, passing several successive rows of new, shiny cars owned by the affluent residents of the fashionable building.

Finally reaching his personal parking space, he carefully backed into the wide spot, making sure plenty of open space surrounded his precious car.

Putting the Saab in park, Laszlo peered expectantly at his phone. Natalia had answered:

"Of course. C U next time."

Laszlo's smile faltered, and he assumed a less happy expression. "Glad you were satisfied, Natalia. Must be my animal magnetism."

Frustrated with the travails of his love life, Laszlo looked up at the corner of the parking garage. Strangely, a light seemed to be broken there, leaving the area dark. Busted lights might be common elsewhere, but in this building, they were virtually unheard of. In fact, he had never seen one of these areas left dark.

Unsure of himself, he felt bothered by...something in the dim corner. Waiting, he stared for some time, letting his eyes explore the area, as if half expecting someone to leap from the area.

Nothing. The shadowy space was empty.

Shrugging, Laszlo rubbed his mustache to bring some of his whiskers under control. Feeling pretty good, he lifted his phone and dialed Erica.

At her apartment, Erica lounged on the couch, an open laptop balanced on her reclined legs. Typing mechanically, she perused the bright screen of her email program.

On the cushion to the side, her phone lit up. Wrinkling her nose, she took some time before answering. Holding it up, she was curt. "Yes. What do you need?"

"I...um, wanted to speak with Monica," said Laszlo, his voice guarded. "I wanted to check how she's doing—to see how her day went?"

Pausing, Erica glanced over to the living room's matching recliner. Monica sat there with a messy ice cream cone, and between licks, she glowered at the phone and the apologetic voice coming from it.

"She doesn't want to talk to you," Erica said. "Do you make it a point to disappoint her? Is this fun for you?"

"Why?" Laszlo asked. "I told you I had meetings I couldn't—"

"She had a bad day at the zoo," Erica said, raising her normally calm voice. "A bunch of monkeys threw food and shit at her."

Sitting up, Laszlo grew concerned. "What? Is she okay? You want me to...come over?"

"She's fine," Erica replied, deliberately ignoring his second question. "But if her father had been there like he promised...."

Laszlo lowered his head, pinching the bridge of his nose between his thumb and index finger. Overcome with shame, he wondered if he had ever done the right thing in his life, particularly regarding his family.

"Tell her I'm sorry," he said, his voice thick with remorse. "Tell her I'll take her to that movie she wanted to see, the one with that ant superhero guy. Think she'll...like that?"

"That film was years ago, Laszlo. Tell her yourself...when she's willing to talk to you."

After a moment of silence, Erica softened slightly. "Just call her tomorrow; I'm sure she'll be open to an apology."

Staring into the garage's shadows, Laszlo's eyes darted around uncertainly. Sighing, his tone grew into a discouraged whine. "Okay, sleep well and give her my love."

The call ended without a goodbye, and Laszlo sighed again. His good mood now gone, he peered again into the unlit corner of the underground garage.

A movement crossed the darkness, and a shadow shifted in the deficient light. A tall figure stood there, barely visible.

Confused, Laszlo tilted his head. Rolling down the window, he called into the quiet, deserted garage, "Who's there?"

No answer came from the silhouette. The shadowed outline tilted ever so slightly, as if whoever was there was assessing him.

Worried, Laszlo switched to Hungarian. "Do you live here?"

Again, no response. Frowning, he rolled up the window and locked the door. Reaching over to the glove box, he rummaged inside, and extracting a flashlight, pressed the button while shaking it.

Glancing up, Laszlo now saw the Huntsman standing only a few feet in front of the car. Shocked, he dropped the malfunctioning light, which clattered to the floor.

The Huntsman's features were obscured in the limited light. His hooded head was covered completely, shrouding his face. He wore odd clothes, like one of those role-players who attend medieval festivals.

The enormous figure leaned on a cane, except the walking stick appeared long, even for such a tall man.

With frightening speed, the Huntsman raised the implement and thrust his dark spear at Laszlo's windshield.

"Oh, fuck," Laszlo shouted, arching his body, trying to get out of the way of the incoming weapon.

The razor-sharp head of the dark weapon pierced the window, sliding into the vehicle's interior.

Terrified, Laszlo screamed as it came straight toward his face.

Chapter Three

Erica sat at the kitchen table, wrapped in a soft robe. Her feet were elevated on another chair, and she concentrated, painting her toenails with surgeon-like precision. Her gaze, locked in an irritated grimace, showed she wasn't enjoying the beauty effort.

In fact, Erica had never been fond of this female ritual, but she had never quite managed to free herself from performing it. Feminine pomp aside, the truth was that it just looked tawdry to leave toenails—or any nails, for that matter—unclean.

It was similar to having hairy armpits or legs. Women had the freedom to sport such an appearance, but that freedom came with both genders thinking you were disgusting if they actually witnessed you looking like a female Bigfoot.

Across the table, Monica munched on a bowl of cereal. Glancing at Erica's pale feet, she moved her skeptical gaze back to her mother.

"Mom, why exactly do we paint our toenails?" Monica asked.

Erica smiled, but the smile faded as she thought more about the question. There was nothing like kids asking questions she should have addressed long ago.

"Good question, Mon. I was just thinking the same thing. I would say it's to look prettier, but it seems like only us girls care about it. I never saw a man focus too much on painted nails. At least, not any man you'd want interested in you."

Thinking harder, Erica smiled as she found a silver lining. "And at least I don't pay someone else to do it."

Looking puzzled, Monica stared out the window, contemplating something. Sunlight from the early morning streamed into the room, making her squint as she worked through her thoughts.

Below, foot traffic was light on the cobblestoned street, and only a fat man with a cane provided any interesting people-watching potential. The plump fellow seemed obsessed with dragging his leg in a peculiar sliding motion as he struggled across the public square.

Finishing up her toes, Erica fanned the resulting ruby-red nails.

Moving her gaze back to her mom, Monica's eyes grew more inquisitive. "Dad didn't like painted toenails? Maybe he would've stayed if you could've...done something else?"

Frowning, Erica didn't answer, and she fixed her daughter with a disapproving glare at the new direction of the conversation. Lowering her feet, she opened her laptop and ignored the question.

Clicking quietly, she brought up another news story about the murdered homeless couple. Scrolling through a few photos of the blood-drenched crime scene, Erica quickly had enough of what passed for current events and closed the computer.

Taking a deep breath, Erica's eyes assumed a contemplative stare before returning to Monica.

"I never did figure out what your father wanted," Erica answered, finally breaking the silence. "I doubt he knows—to this day. Men are funny sometimes."

This didn't seem to be the answer Monica wanted. Frowning, she carried her bowl to the sink and dropped it with a too-loud clink.

Turning to her mother, Monica's expression grew agitated, a clear sign that an argument was coming Erica's way. "That's all you have to say, Mom? Dad's funny?"

Meeting her gaze, Erica chewed her lip, considering where the conversation was heading, as well as whether it was worth participating in. The thing with kids, and especially prepubescent girls, was that when they wanted to argue, there wasn't much that could be done to avoid it.

After a resigned sigh, Erica began to speak in a cross voice. "Look, I don't—"

A strong rap on the door stopped the downward slide of the discussion.

Surprised, Erica stood and stared at the door. "Who could that be on a Saturday morning?"

Pulling her robe tight, Erica moved to the door. Peeking through the peephole, she saw a weary man in a rumpled suit staring at her door. The man was on the far side of his forties, and his dark-circled eyes were intelligent, even as his dour face was serious and noncommittal.

A sense of dread rose in Erica's throat, forcing her to squeak out her words. "Who ...is it?"

The man held up a police badge to the peephole. His slight Hungarian accent was precise and considered, with each word carefully measured. "This is Detective Nemeth from the Budapest Police. May I speak with...Erica Varga?"

Looking quizzically back to her daughter, Erica carefully swung open the door, and her worried eyes moved to Nemeth's.

Behind her, Monica stepped closer to the door, her eyes equally troubled.

"Yes? How can I help you?" Erica said, her voice barely above a whisper.

Nemeth took some time to answer, gazing at mother and daughter for several long moments. Gathering himself, he put on his most clinical and controlled expression. "I am here to discuss Laszlo Varga. Do you have some time? This may take a while."

* * *

Nemeth sat at the kitchen table, leaning over his notebook and peering through clean reading glasses. A cup of steaming coffee was next to him, along with an arrangement of home-frosted cookies.

Sitting across from him was Monica, who stared at Nemeth as he scribbled in a worn notepad. Curious and worried, she nibbled on one of the treats.

Standing in the kitchen and holding her own coffee, Erica watched Nemeth with open anxiety. Glancing between her daughter and Nemeth, she worried about what Monica could hear. "What is happening, Detective?"

Nemeth glanced over the rims of his glasses, considering his words carefully. "Your husband…"

"Ex-husband," Erica interrupted.

Nemeth nodded, scribbling a few notes. "Your ex-husband…has been attacked. Last night."

Alarm filled Erica's face, and she exchanged fearful glances with her daughter. Nemeth noted the genuine surprise in the exchange.

"Is he okay?" Erica asked, setting her coffee on the counter with a shaking hand.

Nemeth took a moment to answer, letting the question hang in the air. The silence left mother and daughter with expectant, horrified expressions. Their eyes widened, agonizing as they waited for a reply.

"Yes, he has not been harmed seriously," Nemeth responded. "He was attacked in his car last night."

At first, relief flowed across Erica's face. But then confusion crept into her features. Focusing on Nemeth, she stepped closer and frowned.

Glancing briefly over at her daughter, Erica's eyes clouded with worry. "In his car? Was he robbed on the street?"

Nemeth paused, weighing his words. His piercing eyes searched her face. "No, he was attacked in his garage…in a most unusual manner."

Staring directly at Nemeth with some hostility, Monica interrupted their interaction by clearing her throat. Looking hostile, the intensity of her glare made Nemeth recoil, as if he hadn't noticed a deadly snake slithering too close for comfort.

Speaking slowly, Monica directed a fierce scowl at Nemeth. "Who tried to hurt my daddy?"

Nemeth took a deep breath, taken aback by Monica's forcefulness. "We don't know yet. The attacker shoved a spear through your father's windshield. He was later found by a neighbor, screaming in the back seat of his car."

Squinting, Erica processed the strange news. Her gaze wandered around the kitchen, as if she was searching for something that could make sense of the weird story.

Sighing, Nemeth stood, straightening out his cheap suit coat and making eye contact with Erica. His gaze lingered, his open-eyed curiosity making her uncomfortable. Continuing the inquisitive stare, he waited expectantly.

"What is it, Detective?" Erica asked, her voice growing defensive.

Nemeth gazed at Erica with a patronizing smile, all the while holding her with his cold, calculating eyes. He avoided looking at Monica, as if doing so might provoke a physical assault.

"Mrs. Varga, I will be honest here. The vast majority of violent attacks carried out in an ambush fashion...are premeditated," said Nemeth, hesitating as he searched for the proper words in English.

Erica motioned her hand in a circle, urging him to get to the point. Meanwhile, her expression grew less cordial.

"And are committed by people known to the victim," Nemeth continued, his eyes boring into hers. "People with an 'axe to grind,' as you Americans say. Jilted lovers, or perhaps even angry ex-spouses. Most often, a man commits these acts, but there are exceptions."

To the side, Monica slapped the table, quickly getting Nemeth's attention. "Are you saying my mom attacked my dad? Are you stupid? She's been here..."

Erica stepped close to Monica, calming her daughter with a gentle hand on her shoulder.

In response, Monica's anger subsided, though her glare remained lively and unafraid.

Erika frowned, moving her exasperated gaze back to Nemeth. "Do you really think I am strong enough to attack Laszlo? With a spear, of all things? Who does something like that? What next? Maybe I'll wait for him at his gym with a poison dart and a blowgun?"

Nemeth couldn't help but smile, briefly picturing Erica crouched by a treadmill, lying in wait with the straw-like weapon.

Nemeth's amusement faded, his face reassuming its stoic interview mode. "It is not so expensive to hire someone to hurt another, Mrs. Varga. Or...to imagine some creative way to threaten a deserving person."

Erica chuckled, her ironic smile unconvinced. Her lack of worry at the insinuation wasn't unnoticed by Nemeth.

But Nemeth continued, ignoring her ridicule. "I am also just doing my job. I have come here to find...the truth."

"Truth, Detective? I'll give you the truth. Laszlo was a horrible husband, so I divorced him," Erica scoffed, motioning to the apartment around them. "And I'm much better off now."

Leaning toward Nemeth, Erica lowered her voice, calming herself. "So, your questions are ridiculous. I have nothing to gain by hurting him—even if he deserves it."

Hesitating, she pointed coolly at Monica. "I also have a daughter with him, who loves him dearly. How could I hurt her?"

Nemeth peered over at Monica, then back at Erica. His face eased as he considered the situation, carefully studying both mother and daughter.

Shrugging, Nemeth acquiesced with a grunt. "Fair enough, Mrs. Varga. If I have offended you, accept my apologies. Finding bad people requires a deliberate approach."

Erica shook her head, again glancing at Monica before returning her gaze to Nemeth. "I don't think you're sorry, Detective. You strike me as a guy who hasn't been sorry about much in your life. In fact, you seem like someone who will do whatever it takes to bring a criminal in, no matter the cost."

Shaking her head, she flashed a sad smile. "But you need to look elsewhere for your spear attacker, because it certainly isn't me."

After a long silence, Nemeth rubbed his chin and nodded. Swigging the rest of his coffee, he stood and pulled on his overcoat. A sheepish smile crept over his face as he prepared to leave.

Tilting her head, Erica suddenly remembered something. Placing her hand on his arm, she stopped his departure.

It was an unexpected move. Surprised, Nemeth looked down at Erica, his eyes probing hers.

Looking over at her daughter, she spoke softly. "Mon, give me and the detective some time alone, would you? We have some adult things to discuss."

Confused, Monica glanced several times between her mom and Nemeth, as if she couldn't understand how she could be excluded from anything. Unhappy, she turned and sulked off to her room.

When Monica's door clicked shut, Nemeth fixed his gaze on Erica, his eyes sharp and unyielding, focusing like a shark on floundering prey.

Nemeth's ongoing glare made Erica uneasy. Stepping back to the counter, she retrieved her coffee, slowly taking a nervous sip of the almost-cold brew.

Raising her eyes, she tried sounding sure of herself. "Those homeless people, the ones I saw on the news"

Nemeth perked up, extracting a notebook from his pocket as Erica's words trailed off.

"I think I ran into them on Wednesday," Erica continued, frowning. "In front of that supermarket at Arena Plaza, where all those stalls are."

Nemeth held up his hand, frowning as he scribbled in his notes. His grave demeanor was serious, his pen darting across the paper as he made copious notes.

Looking up, Nemeth's face flushed red. "Did they say anything to you? Why didn't you contact us?"

Erica lowered her eyes, guilt tugging at the corners of her mouth. "I wasn't sure it was them. I'm still not completely sure, but they really made a lasting impression on Monica and me. They were begging for money, and they weren't polite about it."

Setting down her cup, Erica crossed her arms, her eyes growing distant as she hugged herself. "They scared Monica, so I gave them some cash to leave us alone. I'm not sure if this helps, but since you're here for no reason, maybe it isn't a total waste."

Finishing his notes with a final scrawl, Nemeth scowled. Putting the pad away, he pulled his coat tight and sighed. "People are dead, and you don't tell the police? Is that how things are done in your world, Mrs. Varga?"

"No, Detective. As I said...I'm not even sure it's them. Do you take courses on how to be a jerk? I'm trying to help."

Quiet fell between them as they exchanged wary glances. Neither appeared happy with the other.

Breathing deep, Nemeth was the first to break the awkward silence. Reaching inside his jacket, he pulled out a business card, which was off-white and had the insignia of the Budapest Police Department in gold trim.

Snapping it in front of Erica's eyes, he spoke deliberately. "That isn't an excuse for not telling us sooner."

Setting the card on the counter, Nemeth leaned it against his empty coffee cup, taking time to balance it just right. "If you know anything else or can think of something, please call. For your own conscience, I hope the killer harms nobody else before we catch him."

Erica nodded, trying not to let guilt overwhelm her. Her emotions tugged her in conflicting directions. Part of her wanted to apologize profusely, while another wanted to tell the arrogant detective to drop dead.

Without another word, Nemeth paced to the door and let himself out, leaving Erica to stare at the now-empty apartment. Conflicted, she wondered if any of this was her fault.

Outside, Nemeth walked to the elevator, popped a piece of gum into his mouth, and pressed the button for the ground floor.

As the doors pinged open, his expression remained stoic and unreadable.

The bowling alley buzzed with noisy evening players, and clusters of varied people chatted loudly throughout the busy establishment.

Groups of bowlers crowded tables stacked with french fries and pizzas, shoveling food down between animated conversations. Some licked their fingers free of grease or ketchup, while others wiped their hands directly onto the gaudy shirts of their colorful teams.

From the main entrance, streetlights bled through large glass front doors, and a backdrop of night sky peeked from between weathered buildings across the illuminated street.

The alley had only ten lanes, and in the Hungarian fashion, there was no seating for those waiting to bowl directly near the lanes. People who wanted to relax between frames had to jostle for space near the food tables and assorted spectators, making for a spirited and active venue.

Erica sat at a table among the milling crowd, which was back from the bowling area. Bent over, she tried to squeeze her feet into weathered bowling shoes that just fit over her pink socks. The effort was complicated by knots in the worn shoelaces of the house shoes. Grimacing in frustration, she finally yanked them on and tied the laces.

Around her, the crash of pins heightened the lively energy of the place, and throngs of players screamed in joy at the achievement of an occasional strike or spare. Despite the chaos, the atmosphere was pleasant.

Sitting nearby, Adam Molnar peered at Erica with a grin as he fastened his own shoes into place. Pudgy and with horn-rimmed glasses, he exuded a nerdy vibe, which was offset by his friendly and open face.

Smiling, Erica chuckled and pointed toward their waiting pins. "I haven't been bowling in twenty years. If I manage to hit one pin, I'll be amazed. I could never figure out how people control where it went or what made it hook. Seems almost like voodoo."

Adam grinned, motioning down their lane. Some enthusiasm bled into his tone as he spoke in perfect American English. "Well, I figured you're from the U.S., so I had to be creative with a date. I saw the Bowling World Championship when I went to college in Reno, but I never did figure out how to throw the ball right."

His smile faded a bit, and he glanced tentatively at Erica. "Besides, I needed to lose weight, but I had to find a sport that didn't require actual exercise. So...here we are."

Chuckling, Erica nodded. "Yeah, can't say that I ever saw anyone lose weight from bowling. Can you even call something a sport when most bowlers haven't worked out—like ever?"

Flashing a warm smile, Erica sat down at the lane console. Not technologically inclined, she fiddled with the controls, growing frustrated in little time.

Approaching from behind, Adam leaned over her shoulder and expertly arranged the game by pushing several lighted buttons. At first, Erica was surprised by his closeness, but as he hovered near, she quickly grew more comfortable.

Finishing the effort, Adam stepped back. Moving to the side, he peered down into Erica's dark eyes.

Sounding measured, as if testing the waters, he lowered his voice. "So, tell me, how does a nice American woman end up in Hungary? There aren't many of you over here, and even fewer that are single."

Looking somewhat uncomfortable, Erica shrugged. "I was kind of happily married, so we moved to Hungary to raise our kid in Europe. It seemed like a good idea at the time, moving back to Laszlo's home country, and I thought it'd be good for my daughter to learn some languages and experience other cultures. Nebraska is a great place, but you can't really see the rest of the world there."

Her smile wilted as she glanced around, taking in the smiling faces of happy couples in the surrounding crowd.

"Unfortunately, everything went to shit after we got here. So, I was stuck, and now I have to make the best of it."

"You and your ex-husband couldn't work it out?" Adam asked, obviously glad they hadn't. "You couldn't get counseling or something?"

"That's not really an option when he's got a girlfriend—or two. It makes counseling a hard sell with so many people involved."

Adam nodded but didn't respond. Gesturing down the lane, he collected his ball and made a great show of lining himself up like a professional bowler.

Approaching carefully, he slipped and threw the ball straight into the gutter.

Erica giggled, clapping her hands in mock praise. "My hero. We'll make a great team. We can take turns not scoring."

Adam sauntered back to the ball return, shaking his head. "I'm probably never going to make a living at this."

Furrowing his brow, he tried winking at Erica, but the effect was unconvincing, as his poor eye control made him look a bit like a convulsing pirate.

Frowning, he flexed his fingers over the whoosh of the fan screen.

Glancing back at Erica, his face grew empathetic. "I'm sorry about your divorce. That's a lot to go through for anyone, especially in another country and having a kid."

Pursing her lips, Erica sighed. "It isn't so bad now—we actually get along better. Besides, Monica loves him to death, despite him being a selfish jerk half the time. He's one of those people you can't help but like, however many times he screws up."

Adam nodded, a vague grin filling his face. "I knew a guy like that once, Thomas Hearngrove. He spent years running up gambling debts and not paying back personal loans on time, yet everyone kept giving him chances. He finally moved to Chile, I think, without returning a penny to his legion of fans. To this day, nobody really dislikes him or talks badly about him. Characters like him are worth their weight in gold, if only for their entertainment value."

Erica nodded but didn't respond. Her thoughts drifted to all the times she had given chances to Laszlo with no positive results. It was true that he was likable despite his faults, but that hadn't made her wasted efforts any easier.

She sometimes wished Laszlo had decamped to another location with one of his women; maybe it would have made things easier for both her and Monica. In fact, Chile would probably have been a good option to get him out of her life—if only her daughter didn't still love him so much.

Adam picked up his ball and lined up again. He focused ahead, and this time his poorly thrown ball angled down the lane, then recovered to knock down three pins. Relieved, he grinned at avoiding the dreaded double-zero on the electronic scoreboard.

Erica clapped again, her smile returning.

"What about you?" Erica asked, a flicker of interest crossing her face. "Why didn't you ever get married?"

Shaking his head, Adam's voice grew serious. "My parents were divorced when I was young, and I always told myself I'd never repeat their mistake."

Surprised, Erica raised her eyebrows. Caution was always a smart tactic in life, but cynicism was also a bad way to engage with the world. She knew lots of single people, but the ones that were happy and alone could be counted on one hand, and maybe on just a few fingers.

"Or...I just never met the right woman," Adam suggested, smiling in mock innocence.

In response, Erica clicked her tongue and nodded. "That's a better answer. Nothing ventured, nothing gained. At least that's what I've always told myself about my failed marriage."

Now, Erica looked down at her hands, clasping and unclasping them self-consciously. "The problem with that is, like most clichés, it doesn't really help anything. Have you ever noticed how people tell themselves things to feel better, but then don't actually feel better? Seems like a pointless exercise at this point."

Adam grinned but stayed silent. Keeping an open ear to listen to women was sometimes better than talking too much. Everyone needed someone to hear them, especially when times were tough. At least, that's what his mom always said.

Standing, Erica stepped over to the rack to choose her weapon against the bowling pins.

Collecting a pearly white ball, she carefully positioned herself for her own try at bowling infamy. Breathing deeply, she stared intensely down the lane, as if this precise shot would win her the Professional Bowling Association Championship.

Behind her, Adam's eyes drifted to her attractive posterior. His smile grew wider as he stared, and when she threw her own clacking ball into the gutter, he barely noticed the errant shot.

* * *

The night was quiet beneath the clear sky of Margaret Island. Set in the middle of the Danube River on the north side of Budapest, the island was a hub of recreation for the capital. Its large surface area was covered with grass, trees, and picnic areas, and it usually swarmed with people seeking relief from the rigors of urban life.

But now, the area was largely unoccupied. Several picnic tables were arranged in rows across an open grassy field, and hosts of bugs buzzed around the hazy lampposts located near them.

Above, stars shimmered, and joined together with the moon, they provided glowing illumination for the picnic area.

To the side, branches of numerous trees swayed with a gentle breeze, their rustling limbs sounding like a distant cheering crowd.

At the farthest of the tables, the one closest to the wooded area, two people enjoyed the late-night surroundings. Andreas Horvath sat at a badly maintained wooden table, smiling and relaxed. Holding up a glass of red wine, he swished the deep-red liquid in the faint light.

Across from him sat his wife, Markita Horvath. Stern-looking and in her early fifties, she held her own wine as she met her husband's contented gaze.

Chicken dinners were spread around them, half-eaten and set aside for the moment. Two wine bottles were perched on the table, with one already drained of its contents. Their phones and assorted personal items, brought for the remote dinner, were strewn across the rest of the impromptu picnic area.

Markita raised her glass, a creeping smile replacing her dour expression. "Here's to another year being over, and another summer of relaxation."

Andreas clinked glasses with her before taking a sip. Happy to enjoy the moment, he stayed quiet.

"This is becoming something of an annual celebration for us," Markita continued, glancing around the deserted recreation area. "It's nice to be away from those kids, even if it's only for a few months. God, I hate that school."

"No truer words have ever been said," Andreas responded, gazing with dull eyes over the rim of his glass. "When you have to be around brats for a living, you really must find a way to decompress if you want to keep your sanity. Now, we have almost three months to return to the world of the rational."

After another sip, Markita swallowed and grinned. "Agree. I hate to sound cynical, but I can't understand why people have kids at all. It's like they were invented to destroy the enjoyment of life."

Andreas almost choked on his drink, coughing as he laughed and shook his head. "True, but how else would we get jobs that give us the summers and holidays off, without kids?"

"For that matter, who would do all the crappy manual work in the world if nobody had children?" Markita responded, continuing the silly thought experiment. "If garbage collectors didn't have kids, I might have had to ride around on those dirty trucks myself."

Going silent, Andreas stared up into the night. He really did enjoy his time away from work. "It seems like there's a lot of good reasons to have children, just not a reason for *us* to have them."

Markita put down her glass and scanned the table, evaluating the remains of their recent feast. Standing, she motioned to a trail and some stands of trees to the west. "Shall we take a walk and burn off dinner?"

Nodding, Andreas rose and took her hand. Grabbing the remaining wine bottle, he squinted as he held it up to check the volume.

Gesturing ahead, Andreas led Markita down the dirt trail into the woods. As they moved into the darkness, they were carefree and happy. Walking gingerly into the darker undergrowth, their movements were relaxed and worry-free.

From a copse of trees seventy yards away, the Huntsman watched from another perspective. With an eerie glow coming from the husband and wife, he saw more colors than normal vision allowed. The heat signatures from Andreas's and Markita's upper bodies exuded a reddish glow against the darker background. Their limbs were dimmer, while the surrounding woods and ground retained only a faint residual leftover from daylight.

As Markita and Andreas walked down the pathway, the Huntsman followed, moving his large frame with minimal disturbance through the swaying brush.

* * *

Later, the couple sat cross-legged on a rocky beach of the Danube River. The mellow surface of the river drifted past in a gentle flow, with swirls of water marking varied eddies in the powerful waterway.

It was a large and turbulent river, but its calm pace was soothing in the darkness.

Across from them, the glow of the big city stretched for several hundred yards. Contrasted with their lonely beach, the bright city and its thousands of individual lights shimmered in the darkness, providing bright reflections in the water below. The moment was entrancing, and they absorbed the peaceful scene with relaxed, subdued eyes.

Taking a deep drink from his bottle, Andreas beamed with buzzed contentment. He held out the half-empty bottle to his wife, his glossy eyes enticing her to join him in intoxication.

Markita shook her head, grinning at her husband's booze-addled condition. "No thanks. Looks like I'll be driving us home. I should remember your weakness for wine means we take a taxi ride next year."

Shrugging, Andreas took another hit from the bottle. He grimaced as he swallowed, wishing Markita had bought the more expensive stuff. A teacher's salary only went so far to pay for luxuries, even if the hours and days off were great. *But why do I always have to drink the cheap shit?*

Markita heard a scraping sound behind them and pivoted her head. Suddenly weary, she scanned the tree line, but nothing appeared out of the ordinary.

Nothing moved, and the shadows held no visible threats.

Beside her came a loud *thud*, followed by intense gasping. Alarmed, she stared over, her shocked eyes growing wide.

Andreas had a long shaft sticking from his lower back, and the front of a black spear had run him through, its sharp head buried into the soft flesh of his right thigh.

Oddly, the horrific scene, appearing like an unbelievably wicked dream to her convulsing mind, reminded her of a skewered insect from one of her school science experiments.

One of Andreas's arms spasmed as he tried reaching back to extract the offending spear, while the other pawed at his wife for help. Unable to do either, he looked like a flailing, helpless animal set up to be slaughtered.

"Andreas, what the fuck?" Markita shouted, trying to grab the spear's shaft.

When she grasped it, the weapon's bizarre material cut her hand, and blood spurted from a deep slash in her palm. Her seeping gash quickly mixed her own blood with her husband's draining wound.

She yanked her cut fingers back, disbelief and confusion paralyzing her mind. For the moment, apoplectic shock forced numbness into her limbs.

Grabbing outward, her trembling hands tried again to support Andreas, but her dexterity weakened, forcing her to pull back. Like a blinded and cornered rat, she became aimless, unsure of her options.

Not knowing her path forward, Markita stood and looked at the trees behind her.

To her side, Andreas lulled against her leg, blood spurting from his mouth onto her white pants. Abruptly, he stopped moving and slumped forward, still pinned in his cross-legged stance.

The Huntsman emerged from the trees, walking slowly toward Markita and her mortally wounded husband. As he approached, he drew a black wicked-looking knife from his waist. Strangely, he didn't appear in a great hurry as he strode her way.

"Help me. Somebody help us," screamed Markita, her panicked eyes scanning the empty surroundings.

Even in one of Central Europe's largest cities, no one was there to hear her plea, and no shouts or running feet responded to her cries for help. The echo of her screams continued, even as her attacker paced closer.

Stepping backward, Markita stumbled, leaving her lifeless husband behind.

Panning her head, she searched for an escape, some path to freedom from her horrid circumstance. If she tried fleeing into the woods, she would have to go through the Huntsman, which was not a wise choice.

Trapped, she retreated farther, wading backward into the river's shallows. The water was numbingly cold at her ankles, and she stumbled, just catching her balance on the slick rocks.

As she waded deeper, the water reached her thighs, then her waist, shocking her with its frigid temperature and making breathing difficult. Gasping, she tried to catch her breath, struggling to adjust to the icy temperature.

To her front, the Huntsman stopped next to her silent, still husband. The hulking figure's face was covered under a cloth hood, and he tilted his head at her, almost as if confused.

Markita didn't know what to do. Backing farther into the powerful current, she now treaded deep water and began drifting downstream. Struggling to keep her head above water, she could only stare at the predatory attacker.

Looking back at Andreas, the Huntsman yanked the spear free from his limp body and stuck it deep into the soft earth of the riverbank. Reaching down, he used his vicious knife to slowly sever Andreas' head, wrenching it free with a sickening, sticky sound.

Holding up the grisly trophy by its hair, he peered at Markita as she drifted away, like he was curious where she would be going at such a late hour.

Markita wanted to scream, but the freezing water prevented her from drawing breath. As she floated away, her horrified eyes fixated on the evil assailant as she disappeared into the darkness.

Chapter Four

The apartment was dim, lit by only a single weak bulb over the kitchen table. Adam stood in the living room, squinting up at the photos above the television.

Focusing on Sammy Davis Jr., he gestured toward the famous singer. "Are you a fan of his music?"

In the kitchen, Erica took two beers from the fridge and poured them into waiting glasses. She set the chilled drinks on the table next to a box of greasy pizza.

"Not really. I'm fonder of the seventies and eighties rock," Erica replied. "I just liked his attitude, so he makes a good decoration for the living room."

"His attitude?"

"Yeah. No matter what anyone told him, he did his own thing—and looked cool doing it. I remember once seeing him play a role in a western when I was young. He was a dreadful actor, and to this day, I don't remember the name of the movie. But I thought, 'Anyone who looks that sharp while acting that badly is a hero of mine.' He was kind of like Sinatra; he did things his own way."

Adam grinned and nodded, approving of her logic. Walking to the kitchen, he stared down at the pizza as he accepted the beer from Erica. The melted cheese and greasy pepperoni looked damn tasty, but the idea of gorging himself in front of his new love interest made him hesitate. *Why didn't she get tofu takeout?*

That would've been easy to avoid.

"Well, the date was interesting," Erica said, sipping from her frothy glass. "I never thought I would win a bowling match with a score of eighty-five."

Setting down his drink, Adam finally gave in and detached a slice of stringy pizza from the pie.

Holding it up, he adopted an exaggerated tone, using his best approximation of a gameshow host. "I'd say my loss is because I'm not in good practice, but the truth is I'm just bad at sports. All sports."

With that, Adam performed a flex, pointing the pizza at the ceiling in a mock bodybuilder pose. "In fact, I have yet to find a sport I am good at."

Erica chuckled, amused at the pose and his sense of humor. Grabbing her own slice, she held it up with a flourish. "If you're going to be bad at sports, even bowling, we might as well have another slice of fat."

Down the hall, the sound of a door closing interrupted their banter. Adam and Erica looked at each other like chagrined teenagers.

Holding a finger to her lips, Erica offered a conspiratorial whisper. "Never thought I'd be scared to bring boys home in my thirties."

A toilet flushed, and Monica padded out of the hallway. With sleepy eyes, she focused on the hushed adults with a disapproving gaze.

Frowning, she rubbed the sleep from her eyes. "You guys are as loud as the subway. Why are you being quiet all of the sudden?"

Monica flicked on several switches, and the kitchen erupted in bright light. All three shied away from the intense glow of the bulbs.

Blinking away artifacts in her vision, Erica raised her eyebrows at Monica. "Did you have a good time with Hanna?"

Monica frowned and gave an unenthusiastic nod, like the experience could have been better. "Yeah, and her mom said to tell you I behaved good. Also, she said you need to feed me more. Said I'm too skinny."

Adam chuckled. Monica turned her gaze to him, inspecting him with a sour stare.

Adam's smile faded into a worried look. "I just meant I'd be happy to be too skinny. Can't say I've ever been called skinny, much less too skinny."

Adam then flashed Monica a big grin as a peace offering.

Relenting, Monica faced her mom. "And this is...?"

"Mon, this is Adam, a friend," Erica replied.

Monica responded with a doubtful look. Glancing over at Adam, she began her interrogation. "Adam, what's your job?"

"I...work in internet technologies. IT. It, um, pays the bills."

Flashing a wide grin, he glanced over at Erica. "Makes me a hot commodity on the singles' market."

Erica chuckled, but Monica remained unimpressed. "That's interesting because my mom says you're a friend from work. Do you work at the university? In the social science department?"

Out of his element, Adam glanced at Erica for help.

Taking her cue, Erica sighed. "Adam and I were on a date, and I had a nice time. Be so kind as to say *hi* to him, politely."

Monica considered the situation. Coming to a decision, she showed Adam a faint smile and extended her hand.

Adam took her hand in a gentle grip, returning the gesture with a grin. They shook hands for several moments, sizing each other up across the bright table.

"Nice to meet you, Monica," Adam said, trying his best I'll-be-your-best-friend impression.

Studying him for several moments, Monica nodded. With some reluctance, she wrinkled her nose and motioned toward the hallway. "I'm going back to bed. Don't stay up too late."

Looking upbeat, Erica pointed to the pizza box and grabbed a clean plate from the counter. "Would you like a slice?"

Appalled, Monica shook her head as she turned toward her room. "That's disgusting. Why do Hungarians eat pizza with corn all over it?"

After disappearing down the hallway, her bedroom door closed without an answer.

* * *

The teachers' lounge was busy during lunch hour. The long and dimly lit room housed fifteen tables, and most of them were currently occupied. Vases of plastic flowers and cheap condiments were arranged on each table, looking like they had been there since the 1970s.

Numerous professors chatted across the tables and cafeteria food, gesticulating as they engaged in rather intense and also rather boring discussions. Some of the academics' conversations were rather animated, while others were more subdued. Neither seemed likely to solve the world's problems anytime soon, academic or otherwise.

Amidst the cluster of chattering lecturers, Erica sat alone, staring at her plate and picking at a glob of dark, horrid-looking meat. The strange bit of flesh looked like it had been hacked from a hedgehog, cooked whole, then drowned in mud collected from some putrid gutter.

Scrunching her face in disgust, Erica studied the food's awfulness with almost clinical curiosity. Pursing her lips, she leaned in like a scientist examining an unknown mammalian species.

A shadow blocked the light on her tray, and Erica looked up into the face of Evi.

Evi appeared equally appalled at Erica's meal and sat down while focusing on it. Her eyes stayed locked on the unidentifiable lunch for an extended time.

"It's even worse than usual," Evi said, gesturing to the unknown and perhaps unknowable meat. "Every time I think they reached their worst, the cooks surprise me. This school hires the best academics in Europe, but they use Elmer Fudd to cook the food."

"Yeah, they're not known for creating delicacies here," Erica replied, curling her lip, like she feared the meat might walk off the plate on its own.

"I think it goes further than that. Much further," Evi continued, leaning closer and looking cautiously around.

"How so?" Erica asked.

"Well, Alan—that guy I know from the history department—he was telling me at one time, the cattle in Hungary were the best in Europe. He said the herds were used to export beef continent-wide, even to Turkey."

Erica nodded absently, looking down at her phone and starting to text. Focusing down, she didn't attempt to feign interest in Evi's history lesson.

Undaunted, Evi continued. "So, for hundreds of years, the Hungarians had this incredible meat to share with the world. They were known as the go-to place for it. They were like Maine is now—except for meat, not lobster. Are you listening to me?"

"Yeah, I'm just waiting for your enlightening point," replied Erica, still fixated on her phone.

"For hundreds of years, they got the best beef in Europe," said Evi, pointing at Erica's mystery beef. "And now, all they can get is that sad...thing. Have you tried to buy beef here? It's like they try to make it as horrible as possible. They must compete for the worst beef in the history of the world. It makes rat meat look appetizing."

Texting without interruption, Erica "uh-huhed" in reply.

Frustrated, Evi looked down at Erica's phone. Reading some of Erica's upside-down words, she shook her head. "Oh no, now you went and did it; you fell in love."

"No way, Evi," Erica replied, chuckling. "But I'm happy with the guy I met. It's been a long time since I had someone to talk to."

"Let me see," Evi asked, holding out her hand.

Erica held out her phone. Snatching it, Evi browsed through the screen, her expression growing more disgusted with each swipe of the screen.

After perusing the device, she handed it back to Erica.

Evi wrinkled her nose, as if the notion of a relationship was similar to the stench of rancid food. "I tell you to get some meat. I show you some fine pics, and you give me...family photos of some chubby dude."

Overwhelmed, Evi put a finger in her mouth, making a gagging motion.

Unoffended, Erica smiled at the gesture. "Adam is so nice...and understanding...and smart. Did you know he is considered the best in his field in all of Budapest?"

Evi shook her head, looking depressed. "You're a lost cause. I was going to make you my wing woman for life, but instead, I'll be doing happy hour alone. Again. You are a destroyer of my dreams."

Still smiling, Erica put her phone away and returned to the enigma that was her lunch. Keeping a contented smile, she glanced up at Evi.

Glad to see her friend happy, Evi winked at Erica as she took the first bite of her wilted lettuce.

* * *

Getting out of the taxi, Monica stared up at the dilapidated hospital. With tattered stucco and unwashed bricks, the ratty building awaited her visit.

If it had been empty, the structure would have made a good abandoned haunted house. Its unwashed exterior accentuated windows that held panes of opaque glass and streaks of dirt.

Monica took a deep breath and trudged ahead, swinging a plastic bag in her hand as she angled toward the main door.

From outside, the hospital's dreary-looking entrance was only half lit. Multiple lights above the main door flickered and buzzed, clearly needing replacement.

An ambulance idled in front of dirty glass windows to the side of the main entrance, and disinterested EMTs didn't appear rushed as they wheeled an old man into the front lobby on a clattering gurney.

The despondent man on the creaking stretcher looked distraught, his expression saying it all: *Please don't let this be my last visit.*

Monica gave the elderly man a sympathetic nod as she passed by.

Inside, the emergency room was no better. Groups of sickly people took turns looking around the unappealing interior, their worried eyes scanning dirty corners and tiles laid down during the time of the Vietnam War.

The walls were pocked with peeling paint, and the occasional cough of an ailing patient was the primary sound to greet new visitors. Music to lighten the mood seemed to have been left out of the medical budget.

Nodding at an inattentive guard, Monica turned down one of the brighter hallways. Her shoes squeaked on the dingy floor as she passed several more gurneys, where idle patients waited for treatment. Some cried or sobbed from pain and anguish, while others stared blankly at nothing in particular.

Stopping in front of door *17*, Monica smiled, trying to appear positive as she got ready to enter. Inhaling deeply, she brushed stray hairs from her face, put on a sincere smile, and eased the door open.

The room inside had only one bed, a simple one arranged at a weird angle away from the window. It was aligned so that its occupant could see anyone who entered.

Light from a streetlamp outside sent tempered illumination through the window into the shadowy confines of the too-dark room.

Dressed in a white hospital gown, Laszlo lay on the simple mattress with rumpled covers piled around him. Color was missing from his complexion, and he didn't look well.

But his fatigued face brightened considerably when he saw his daughter. "Sweetie, how are you? I'm glad you could come."

Grinning, Monica rushed to his side, her worried eyes tearing up as she hugged him across the bed.

As Laszlo clutched her in his embrace, he glanced at the door, apprehension filling his troubled features.

Pulling back, Monica wiped her eyes and gave her dad a reassuring grin. "Dad, I heard you weren't home yet, so I came to visit."

"I'm okay, sweetie, just had a bit of a scare. This city gets crazier every year."

Perplexed, Monica tilted her head. "What happened? They said some crazy guy attacked you?"

Laszlo's eyes glazed over as he recalled his encounter. "Yeah, a crazy guy, like nobody I ever saw. Some kind of freak dressed in weird clothing. Old stuff I've never seen before."

"You mean, like old Roman sheets or something?"

Laszlo shook his head, snapping out of his brief daydream. "No, not that old. Something you'd see in a painting, like from Caravaggio or someone from the 1500s."

"Caravaggio...?"

"Yeah, I didn't know who he was either. I found him on the internet when I was trying to place the clothes he was wearing."

Monica didn't respond, continuing her confused look as she tried to mouth the famous painter's difficult name.

"And his eyes," Laszlo continued. "It was kind of dark, but I couldn't see his eyes. He had this Harley-type biker beard, but...his eyes."

Laszlo glanced back toward the door, continuing his paranoid focus on the doorway. "I asked the hospital if I could stay another day. I didn't feel like hanging out at my apartment. Good thing it only took a few thousand forints to get it approved."

Glancing across the room, Monica spied a chair. Shrugging, she dragged it over to the side of the bed. Sitting, she set her plastic bag on the covers between them. Inside were candy bars and all varieties of junk food.

"I'll stay with you, Dad. I brought some snacks," Monica said, and she motioned at the television on a mount in the corner. "And we can watch TV. I hear there's a soccer match between Denmark and Hungary. Maybe we'll finally win a game."

Looking relieved, Laszlo stared at his daughter. With his eyes growing watery, he hugged her again.

Chapter Five

Frustrated, Erica got down on her knees. Contorting her face, she reached under the bed, grunting from the effort of stretching so far under it. Her fingers nudged a box wedged behind some Christmas decorations, and with some effort, she finally grabbed its cardboard handle.

"Aha," said Erica, yanking the box from under the bed.

Around her, the room was brightly lit, with a king-size bed and matching mahogany dressers filling the space. The floor was an off-white tile and was covered with a fluffy gray rug, while dishes of cat food and milk were arranged in the corner.

On the wall were two posters; on one was the famous photo of the flag raising on Iwo Jima, and the other showed a view of a roller coaster with a snapshot of Laszlo, Erica, and Monica raising their arms raised in rapt terror. A Post-it note, colored with a black marker, was taped over Laszlo's face.

On the bed, a fat orange cat watched Erica with lazy eyes. The animal appeared comfortably contented in its relaxed pose.

Pulling a bottle of wine from the cardboard box, Erica held it up to admire the vintage. With admirable control, the cat yawned, adopting the universal indifference of felines.

Frowning at the spoiled animal, Erica made a mental note to buy cheaper cat food next time she went shopping.

Excited, Erica paced from the room and moved down the hallway, soon emerging in her familiar living room.

Sitting on the couch, Adam watched the news intently. With one leg crossed over his knee, he looked relaxed with his surroundings, and Erica smiled approvingly.

"I've been saving this for, well, any reason," Erica said, appearing confused. "Hungary has some of the best red wine in the world, so it's not hard to find good quality, but I could never figure out why it's cheaper and better than American wine. You'd think they'd import it to the US and sell tons of the stuff."

To the side, the television showed the Budapest Zoo, which had multiple police cars parked along the curb in front of its wide front gate.

Preoccupied with the images, Adam didn't respond. Instead, he raised the volume on the remote, and a broadcaster's gravelly voice filtered into the room.

"It is not known how many have been mutilated, but zoo officials indicate that numerous animals have been killed in this barbaric attack on these defenseless creatures. The police and the zoo both ask that anyone with information on who perpetrated these crimes immediately come forward..."

Adam muted the sound and looked over at Erica. Queasy, he shook his head at the TV, unsure of what to say.

Wrinkling her nose. Erica joined him in disgust. Gesturing toward scenes of covered animal carcasses, she kept her voice flat. "What the hell is that about?"

Erica was surprised they would transport dead animals this way, as if they were people. But she supposed zoos had their rules. Everyone had rules, even animal morticians—or whoever it was that handled mutilated wildlife.

Adam didn't respond. He continued shaking his head, working through what something so bizarre must mean.

Sighing, he finally turned away from the news. "It's a matter of marketing and supply. Even though the wine is one-third the price and demonstrably better, nobody in the US is interested because this country hasn't branded itself to sell wine. Also, most wineries here can't supply the volume required to export it into such a large market."

Surprised, Erica took a moment to grasp what he was talking about. Realizing the change of topic from her earlier comments about wine, she finally nodded.

Intrigued, Erica walked to the kitchen and uncorked the bottle. Taking two wine glasses from the cabinet, she carefully began pouring. As the dark liquid splashed into the crystal, Erica contemplated the wine issue and the difference in pricing.

"Well, I guess that's our gain then. Now I understand why I never see American wine in stores."

Delivering a glass to Adam, she lowered her voice and gestured out the window to the wider city. "Monica called to say she'll be staying at the hospital with her dad. Then, he'll take her to his place when he checks out."

Worried, Adam licked his lips and glanced around the apartment, like he felt cornered.

"So, we have the place to ourselves," Erica continued. "With no interruptions."

Adam smiled bashfully, unsure where this was going.

"Adam, relax. I don't bite, and I certainly don't fool around on a second date," Erica said, and she dropped next to him with a playful smile.

"Oh, I didn't think—" replied Adam.

"You want to watch a movie?" Erica asked, letting the matter drop. "I've got a whole catalog of 'em here."

Erica reached down and pulled up a large DVD holder from under the coffee table. "What do you like? Just about everything I have is—"

A sharp rap on the front door interrupted her. After a short delay, several more hurried knocks followed.

Frowning, Erica stood and looked quizzically at the door, then down at Adam.

"Who is it?" called Erica.

Detective Nemeth's voice answered from the hallway, his tone strained. "It's me, Mrs. Varga, Detective Nemeth. I need to talk to you."

"I have company, Detective," Erica said, irritation creeping into her voice. "I can come down tomorrow to chat—wherever you are."

Nemeth raised his voice, leaving no doubt about the urgency. "It can't wait, Mrs. Varga. I'll try to be brief, but it's very important."

Perplexed, Erica walked carefully to the door and opened it.

Standing in the hallway was Nemeth, looking grave and holding a briefcase. Three policemen, all dressed in tactical gear, stood beside him. Each of the officers had MP-5 machine guns slung across their chests. None of the group appeared happy to be making a late-night house call.

Shocked, Erica's eyes widened. Shifting her gaze between them, she evaluated her reluctant visitors.

* * *

The kitchen table was laid out with a tray of cookies and an assortment of drinks and coffee. Adam sat with his elbows on the table, clearly distressed as he peered up at the policemen. His previously relaxed demeanor had vanished.

Across the table sat Nemeth, his eyes bleary and bloodshot. Peering down at his notebook, he scribbled some notes, then glanced between Adam and Erica.

Standing in the kitchen, Erica returned his gaze with an unhappy, scrunched-up face. Caught between worry and dread, she appeared expectant, as if waiting for good news that she knew in her heart would never arrive.

In the living room, Nemeth's SWAT companions stood vigilant. Steely-eyed and imposing, they scanned the apartment windows, as if they soon expected someone to burst through the exterior glass.

Breathing deep, Erica grabbed a bag of chips and poured them into a bowl on the table.

Trying to sound cheery, she addressed Nemeth. "This must be bad? Did you catch the guy who attacked Laszlo?"

Nemeth shook his head. Speaking firmly, he stared directly into Erica's eyes. "No. But we discovered the man who attacked your husband is a vicious killer."

"Wha...how...what are you talking about?" Erica exclaimed, disbelief filling her face.

Nemeth stared at Adam impassively.

After a moment, Adam took the hint. Standing, he motioned at the door. "I need to go, um, get back to my apartment. My mom is coming tomorrow, so I should get ready...."

As Adam trailed off, Erica moved close, leaning in and pecking him on the cheek. "I understand. Can I call you when things clear up here?"

Surprised by the kiss, Adam hesitated for a moment. Returning her gaze, he nodded, though his response could never have been described as enthusiastic.

Caught between bizarre circumstance and self-preservation, he had the unmistakable look of a man who preferred safety over a life of police visits and possible murderers.

"Sure, please do that," Adam said, and hurrying to the living room, he collected his coat from the sofa's padded arm.

Stopping at the front door, Adam glanced back before exiting with a bashful smile, looking like a man who had just avoided prison. His retreat was swift and authoritative, if not exactly smooth.

Erica frowned at his departure, but she couldn't blame him for leaving. Bodies and homicide had a way of killing romantic inclinations.

Returning her attention to Nemeth, she lost all semblance of happiness. "Please, spit it out. I think my night is about to get a lot worse."

Nemeth rubbed his stubbled jaw, taking his time to speak clearly. "Those homeless people killed a few days ago were murdered by the same man who attacked your husband."

Surprised, Erica paused to think, though this time she didn't correct Nemeth about her marital status with Laszlo. "And do you think I killed them too, in addition to paying someone to harm Laszlo?"

Nemeth waved her off. "Mrs. Varga, I don't think you did anything. But whoever is doing these things is connected to your family. Of that, there is little doubt."

Erica felt her confusion deepen with each passing moment. Running her fingers through her hair, she held out her hands, peering at her suddenly clammy fingers as she rubbed her knuckles. "Please, go on,

Detective."

"There was blood on Mr. Varga's windshield that matched one of the homeless victims," said Nemeth, speaking in his same matter-of-fact tone. "And they were indeed the same homeless people you saw at Arena Plaza on the day they were killed. We have video from the cameras there."

Nemeth took a swig of his coffee, grimacing at the brew. "We also have camera footage of the killer near the first murder scenes and at Mr. Varga's apartment building. It's the same person in each circumstance. Same clothing and same strange appearance."

Erica's eyes widened. "First murders? Who else has been killed?"

Nemeth glanced at the other officers before refocusing on Erica. Some empathy crept into his voice as he continued. "Mrs. Varga, your daughter's teacher, Andreas Horvath, has been found murdered. His body was discovered on Margaret Island. It's a gruesome crime, one that matches the way the homeless were killed."

"What are you telling me, Detective?" Erica asked, her voice growing shrill. "I just saw him on the last day of school."

Nemeth opened his notebook and scribbled several notes. "You saw him at school?"

"Yes, when I dropped Monica off," explained Erica, disbelief filling her voice. "He was at the front door of the school, greeting the kids as they entered."

Nemeth nodded, finishing his writing. Snapping the notebook shut, he met Erica's eyes. "Also, Mr. Horvath's wife is missing. We're hoping to find her soon."

Nemeth's sour expression made it clear he had zero confidence in the search for the wife turning out with a happy ending.

Sighing, Nemeth lifted his briefcase to the table and popped it open. Withdrawing a folder, he revealed a series of large photos. Grimly, he laid the first three in front of Erica.

The first pictures were booking photos of the homeless, taken while they were alive, and the next showed their bloodied bodies hidden under sheets on the ground in the infamous alley where they were killed.

Nemeth next placed two more printed photos on the table. The first was a smiling school photo of Andreas Horvath, probably taken from a school yearbook. The second showed a corpse under a bloody sheet at a beach on Margaret Island.

Horrified, Erica stared at the ceiling, struggling to process the traumatic events.

"Why are you showing me these...things?" she asked, her tone bordering on hysterical. "Who would do this? What do...I or my family have to do with this?"

Nemeth's deadpan gaze didn't flinch or waver. He peered directly at her, his stare unbothered.

"Mrs. Varga, please listen to me, carefully," Nemeth said, his tone rising. "This is Hungary, a small and peaceful country. We rarely have these kinds of crime here. Small crimes, yes. Pickpockets. Occasional brawls or muggings, that sort of thing."

Nemeth pointed out the window, growing angry. "Some crazy person killing people with a spear is a very big deal here. As you can imagine, my bosses want this solved immediately and this lunatic locked up."

Softening his tone, he continued, "Whoever is doing this is connected to your family; this much is obvious."

Nemeth held up three fingers. "We have three bodies, in addition to the attack on Mr. Varga. All of which are somehow connected to you. Somehow."

Nemeth now leaned carefully over the table, coming very close, imploring her with his eyes. "So, I need you to help me figure out who this crazy person is—before he kills anyone else tied to you or your family."

Feeling detached from reality, Erica looked away from Nemeth. Her eyes roamed the apartment, struggling to make sense of what was happening. After glancing at each of the other officers, she looked back at Nemeth.

Chewing on her lip, she nodded to him. "What can I do?"

Reaching again into his folder, Nemeth extracted two more photos and laid them on the table. Both images showed a bizarre sign of a triangle within a circle. One was scrawled in blood on the dirty bricks of an alley wall, while the other was marked over a *No Camping* sign near a picnic table.

"What's this?" Erica asked, her face knotted in confusion.

"These are the marks the maniac left in the alley and on the island," Nemeth explained. "As far as we can tell, it's some kind of medieval symbol. It's my hope that you know something about this? Or could you check at the university with a colleague? Someone must know what they could mean."

Nemeth took a final photo from the folder and gently laid it down. It was the image of the killer, taken from CCTV.

The man was tall and looked...odd. An old, tattered hood surrounded his head, and a bushy white beard was the only identifiable feature puffing from under the cloth. What was visible of his skin was strangely dark, even in the limited light of the nighttime camera.

"I've never seen clothes like that, they're positively archaic," said Erica, placing her fingers on the photo.

Nemeth looked quizzically at her, then nodded in understanding. "Yes, they are old-style clothes, at least several hundred years by our estimate. We think it's connected to the signs he's marking out at the murder scenes."

Erica turned away from the pictures, thinking through the problem as she struggled with the hideous crime. Images of gore and violence were not something she was accustomed to, and finding that she was now somehow involved with this madness made the nauseating effect much worse.

Lapsing into deep thought, she spoke over her shoulder to Nemeth. "Can I have the photos of this...symbol? I'll see what I can find out."

"Of course, it's why I brought them," answered Nemeth. "They're already publicly available on the internet, in any case. Secrecy is not an easy thing when a scared city is looking for answers. Just make sure to contact me the moment you find anything."

Nemeth motioned to the heavily armed policemen who had managed to creep closer to the table. They each held half-eaten cookies, chewing happily on the snacks. In unison, they stopped when they noticed Nemeth's sudden attention.

Frowning, Nemeth shook his head. "These officers, or others, will be with you at all times until we solve this...problem. So, I suggest you stay here most of the time. It will be easier to ensure your security."

Nemeth packed up the folder and photos in his briefcase, setting aside the requested ones for Erica as he tucked the rest away. "And there are three more officers at Mr. Varga's apartment. I'll have a car pick up your daughter and bring her back tonight. You'll want to keep her close as well."

Nemeth stood straight, arching his back into a stretch. Fatigued, his stooped-over bearing put a decade on his appearance.

Erica turned to meet his gaze, and his always-vigilant eyes focused on her, revealing a caring if controlled temperament.

"Be careful, Mrs. Varga, and please think of anything that might link your family to this killer. Whoever is doing this won't stop. The killer's actions belong to someone who wants to show us something. We just have to listen to what his insane mind is telling us."

Nemeth breathed deeply, shaking his head and wrestling with that idea. "But...I don't need any more bodies to listen to what he has to say."

* * *

The office was large and well organized. Several filing cabinets were spaced at intervals along off-white walls, and orderly desks were positioned between them, creating semi-private areas around the interior of the room.

Artistic renditions of famous Roman artwork lined many of the walls, giving the space a historical, lively feel, with glossy prints of Julius Caeser peppered among images of the Roman Colosseum and the ruins of Pompeii.

Evi sat at a desk in the corner, at a place that offered the most privacy. Looking happy, she held a mischievous grin as she pecked away at her keyboard.

Above her desk hung a calendar featuring various men, half-clothed and oiled for the theme of beefcake adoration.

On her computer, a chat window was open, and as she clacked away, she grew more excited with each typed word.

"Are you sure you can handle me, big boy?"

Waiting for a reply, Evi licked her lips in anticipation. The "Broadbill is typing" indicator lit up, and she anxiously awaited Bill's response.

Finally, his reply appeared:

"Hell yes! I'll bring my boyfriend along and we'll really get going!"

Evi's smile faded, and after an extended sigh, she reluctantly closed the chat program.

Speaking to herself, she shook her head in disappointment. "Too freaky, even for me."

At the entrance to her office, she suddenly noticed Erica waiting to be noticed. Her mood brightened again.

"Girl, good to see you," said Evi, her disappointment quickly forgotten. "Get in here; we got things to talk about."

Stepping into the office, Erica couldn't hide her sour attitude. She tightened her lips into a controlled frown, clearly unhappy at being there.

As she got close, Evi saw the reason for Erica's reluctance; a heavily armed cop, beefy and serious, followed her in.

The officer nodded self-consciously at Evi, then turned to face the office entrance. Outside, several staff members walked by in the hallway, staring at the cop like he was an alien.

Hurrying to Evi's desk, Erica peered down at her friend. She spoke softly, as if quiet words could somehow reduce the impact of the bizarre situation. "Did you find that information we discussed?"

Evi nodded but continued staring at the back of the bodyguard officer.

"Evi?"

Coming to her senses, Evi blinked and reached into a drawer. Pulling out a notepad, she copied information in flowing scrawls onto a blank sheet of paper.

Folding it, she held it up to Erica. "Please tell me this isn't about your new boyfriend."

Taking the sheet, Erica smiled sadly and shook her head. Pausing, she shrugged before answering. "I wish it were something like that. I really do."

Leaning closer, Erica dropped her voice to a whisper. "I've already cleared it with the administration, but I'll be taking some time off. A leave of absence, until stuff gets less crazy in my life."

Evi stared up at Erica, completely lost. At this point, if Erica admitted she was JFK's long-lost granddaughter, Evi wouldn't have been surprised.

"I can't tell you what's going on, but when it's over, I'll tell you everything," Erica said, reaching down to squeeze Evi's shoulder. "And we can finally do happy hour, like we should've done a long time ago. You were right; I should have learned to live a little better, even if it just meant spending more time with friends."

Evi nodded, unable to speak. Holding her gaze, trying to read Erica's thoughts, she stayed quiet.

Smiling, Erica turned and exited the office, waving over her shoulder on the way out.

As Evi watched the officer follow her friend out, a brief but important thought crossed her mind: *I wonder if that cop is single?*

* * *

Laszlo stood at the panoramic window, looking down at the wide plaza below. Fearful, he focused on a pair of policemen guarding the entrance to his upscale apartment complex.

All around the cops were pedestrians and residents of the area, strolling by and following their daily lives, oblivious to the drama Laszlo found himself trapped in.

Raising his gaze, Laszlo scanned the windows of nearby buildings around his complex, places that were also affluent and full of people intent on living good lives.

Studying the lights of the other terraces, he wondered if his attacker could be inside. Perhaps he was being watched even now, by those same bizarre eyes that had sought him in his car in the basement, eyes from a person who wanted to bury a spear into his face.

Frustrated, he stepped away from the window and moved his gaze to the TV on the wall. The faces of his daughter's dead teacher and his missing wife, both looking healthy from humble personal photographs, haunted him on the news. Their smiling images from happier times seemed to blame him for their current problems. *We're dead, Laszlo. What did you do to cause this?*

Bothered and fearful for himself and his family, Laszlo moved carefully to his black leather couch and sat. Fighting feelings of acute unrest, he glanced over at his kitchen table, where his weary gaze fell on his black-and-white pet, a chubby kitty who stared back with detached disinterest. Titling its head, the animal seemed to size him up, almost challenging Laszlo to chase him from his perch.

As if to accentuate its indifference, the spoiled animal began to bathe itself with looping licks of his soft fur.

Stopping himself, Laszlo considered the wisdom of getting the obnoxious pet. He and Erica always kept a cat, and maybe it would have been better to stop the tradition when he became single?

Shaking his head, Laszlo looked around at the rest of the apartment. The place was something of an ideal bachelor pad: spartan, functional, and attractive, it was also easy to maintain. Nobody was here to complain about what wasn't right or to needle him for his bad habits. Here he could go about his business on his own terms, without stress or nagging.

Life should have been perfect, but of course, it was decidedly not. With a failed marriage and a deeply loved daughter he spent half his time neglecting, it was little wonder this expensive place didn't shine as brightly as it should.

Struggling with thoughts of shame, Laszlo blinked away memories of his past sins. Feeling sorry for himself was one thing, but murders and mayhem? Laszlo had never physically hurt anyone in his life. *What the fuck is going on? Who did I piss off?*

Shrugging off self-pity, Laszlo reached for his drink on the Ikea coffee table that fronted the couch. Pulling close the Cola Light, the European version of Diet Coke, he grimaced after taking a sip. Even after adding a lemon slice, the stuff still tasted like crap.

It seemed in Hungary, they held a contest to determine how badly they could botch the Diet Coke recipe. If not for his blood sugar, he would have tried the full-flavored version, but the truth was it was also pretty awful.

Hungary, Budapest specifically, was sort of heaven on Earth: beautiful, relatively cheap, and with loads of gorgeous women and tons of things to do. *Why can't they get the good Coke? Is it some sort of corporate conspiracy?*

Frowning, Laszlo stood and walked to the kitchen table. Scratching the feline's neck, he was rewarded by a self-serving mewl from the little parasite.

Sighting the refrigerator, Laszlo stepped gently toward the too-expensive appliance, grasping the handle of the stainless exterior.

Swinging open the door, Laszlo saw that the inside was full of Chinese food and a box of aged pizza. On the bottom shelf, his expectant eyes found the most important contents.

The mother lode of enjoyment was there: Still in the plastic bag from the local store, a dozen expensive German beers awaited his attention.

These were the types he had cradled and enjoyed his whole life. Through thick and thin, they were the one friend that always gave him exactly what he wanted—exactly what he needed. Now that his life was going to shit, what harm could it do to hug an old friend?

Smiling and holding the refrigerator open, he heard the pinging from the cold box reminding him to shut the door.

Standing still, Laszlo continued to stare at the waiting beer, fighting the urge to reach for a little relaxation.

Chapter Six

The interior of the taxi was clean, with all its seats and dashboard covered in a glaze of freshly wiped disinfectant. The smell and atmosphere were nice, presenting a citrusy, sterile environment to any rider concerned about germs.

Patrik Lakatos was one who fit that profile perfectly, and he stared approvingly around the interior of the Volkswagen cab.

Dressed in a white suit that had seen decades of use, his professorial manner was accented by thick glasses and a perfectly tied blue bow tie. He was a plain-featured and unremarkable man, and although not seriously overweight, his middle-aged physique could best be described as mushy.

Driving the taxi was Ali El Kordi, who was as sharp and immaculate as the interior of his well-groomed vehicle. Even his photo, perched on the dashboard next to a framed stack of business cards, was from a custom photo shoot and emphasized his beaming smile.

El Kordi glanced with a clear gaze into the rearview mirror. His grin was wide and sincere, and his English accent was impeccable. "If you need a ride at any time, I am the man to call. Please do not hesitate to avail yourself of my services. Whatever your needs, I am the man for the job, particularly if proper customer service is a requirement."

Visibly impressed, Patrik nodded down to the driver's business card, which the man had quickly presented when he first entered the cab. Turning it over in a clean handkerchief—always within easy reach to handle such items—Patrik decided on the spot this would be his driver whenever the need for a cab arose in the future. A good customer service experience was rare in the city, almost as rare as a clean cab.

"Ah, here we are, one of the most beautiful sights in Budapest, Saint Stephen's Basilica," El Kordi said, speaking in a voice that would probably have fetched top dollar as a cultured tour guide. "That will be nine thousand forints, payable in either cash or credit."

Patrik smiled as the car stopped at the curb near the magnificent cathedral. Tipping the driver well, he exited the vehicle into the bright and noisy day.

His happiness quickly faded as his face morphed into a fearful stare. Carrying a heavy book bag slung over his shoulder, his gaze flitted from side to side, searching for something through crowds of wandering tourists.

The area around the Basilica was busy, but the mass of pedestrians was unobtrusive. Families made up the main part of the throngs around him, but plenty of sauntering singles were also mixed in with the milling crowd.

The impressive cathedral itself had two towers flanking enormous stone steps, and the main entrance faced a large square that held strolling groups and tourists. Though less than two centuries old, the massive church appeared both ancient and fitting for an old-world neighborhood.

Near the wide-open square were numerous cafés and restaurants, all set up to charge double the price for the pleasure of dining in such an attractive area. Patrik's eyes roamed the series of establishments, searching for his precise destination in the lively area.

At the distant end of the row of eateries, Erica raised her hand to get Patrik's attention. Smiling, she looked happy to see him.

Relieved, he hurried toward her, using his handkerchief to wipe sweat from his balmy forehead. Dodging young children, he kept his attention focused on Erica, noting that she was sitting alone in a chair among several empty tables.

But other matters quickly drew his attention. As he drew closer to Erica, he noticed numerous groups of policemen standing watch around the area. Taking notice of his approach, the officers' location and wary glares suggested Erica was the reason for their presence.

Erica waved as he came closer. Flashing a broad smile, she beckoned him forward, but there was also reservation in her demeanor, like she was surprised that he had actually come.

Noticing her apprehension, Patrik wasn't reassured, and he frowned as he came near the table.

"Mr. Lakatos?" Erica asked, appearing kind as she gestured to the seat opposite her.

Patrik didn't answer as he lowered himself into the clean plastic chair. Instead, he offered Erica a gloomy nod. His timid face, overheated and worried, didn't inspire confidence.

Frowning, Erica motioned to a carafe of coffee, hot water, several pitchers of juice, and a tray of cookies on the table. "Please, have something. Would you like coffee or tea?"

"Yes, please," Patrik replied, a slight English accent just noticeable. "Err... coffee, with sugar if you have it."

Carefully filling a cup with the steaming brew, she spoke slowly, her voice measured. "Thank you for coming, Mr. Lakatos. It's good to meet you."

"Just Patrik is fine. I have never been one to appreciate formality," he replied, nodding his thanks and taking her hand in a limp handshake. "The world would be a better place if we all learned to take one another as we are—without undue formality or ego."

Erica tilted her head, a considered grin crossing her face. Letting go of Patrik's soft hand, she hid her disappointment at his flaccid shake. It may not have been fair, she realized, but a man with a weak handshake rarely inspired confidence—from either gender.

"I think the same. But I must say I appreciate you coming. This is a hard matter to discuss with everything that's going on," she said.

Patrik met her eyes calmly, weighing his words as he stirred several spoonfuls of sugar into the coffee.

"Yes, it is. I had to convince myself to come here. I'm decidedly not a police officer."

Erica flashed a sincere smile, trying to appear upbeat. "Neither am I, but I'm thankful for your efforts. I need help to stop a murdering maniac."

Hesitating, Patrik removed his glasses and used a freshly produced handkerchief to clean his already-spotless lenses. Sliding the spectacles back on, he used a separate handkerchief to wipe an emerging sheen of sweat from his face.

Sighing, he set his bag on the table. Pulling out a leather portfolio, he withdrew a folder and set it on the table. Opening it, he revealed a stack of mismatched papers. "I got all the scans you sent me, and I did a great deal of research. More than I would normally agree to, but this is an interesting case."

From above, the bells of the church began clanging from the tower. The bonging continued for an extended period, and Patrik and Erica, as well as their protective detail, flinched and exchanged nervous glances, as if the interruption could signal something more sinister.

When the sounds died away, Patrik dabbed his forehead and neck again with his soon-to-be-soaked handkerchief.

"It took me three days, and I have to say you have got yourself involved in some very nasty business," Patrik said, a deep frown settling over his features. "The symbols, the ones in blood, seem to come from an old secret society from the 1600s."

"The 1600s?"

"Yes. The society was called the Order of Vengeance. They based themselves on a group from four centuries earlier called the Nizaris."

"Why does that sound familiar?" Erica asked, confused.

"They were the people that coined the term assassin," Patrik explained. "They carved a mountain kingdom out of Persia and Syria in the latter part of the 1100s."

Erica crossed her arms, perplexed. "They came from the Middle East?"

"The original group did. These Nizaris got much of what they wanted by covert murder, using poison, daggers, that sort of thing, to kill their opponents. They were feared throughout their area, by kings and commoners alike."

Erica took a moment to absorb the information, puzzling over the relevance of details from almost a thousand years earlier. "So how did this later Order of Vengeance develop? And why?"

"Well, they got started during the time of the Ottoman occupation of Hungary," Patrik responded. "The Turks occupied much of this country for the better part of two centuries, and this order was created to fight them. They would kill and decapitate at will, killing whoever was an authority. Their raids and ambushes of Ottoman officials were legendary."

"Decapitate?" Erica asked, her eyes narrowing.

Glancing to the side, Patrik became distracted by a loud wedding party on the steps of the cathedral. Several women and men, all dressed in suits and attractive dresses, flaunted the happy occasion with boisterous photographs and celebratory shouts.

Gulping, Patrik continued, "Yes, they would take the heads of their victims, then display them prominently to warn anyone who might willingly cooperate with the occupiers."

Erica nodded, a sour grimace filling her face. "And...are they still around? This group? Would they still be doing these things...hundreds of years later?"

"No, of course not," Patrik responded, but his eyes told a different story, as if unsure of who would do what. "They were only around for a few decades."

Leaning back, Patrik motioned to the imposing cathedral, raising his voice. "The Church accused them of sorcery or some such nonsense. It seems that there were more than just Turks turning up without heads. All manner of people, Christian and otherwise, started being killed. It was a bit of a free-for-all."

"So, what happened to this Order, these more modern assassins?" asked Erica, looking less happy with each answered question.

"The Church declared them diabolical. They were executed to the last man, without mercy or hope of sentence commutation," Patrik said, his face growing grim. "It would appear they exhausted their goodwill with the Church hierarchy. At least, that's what the documents say."

Withdrawing a paper from his folder, Patrik set it in front of Erica. Leaning forward, she stared down at the photocopy.

The image showed a castle in the background. In a square in front of it, several bloody corpses with no heads were stacked, while another man was about to have his head cut off. Holding an axe above the soon-to-be victim, a robed figure was prepared to deliver the fatal blow.

Alongside the scene was a crowd that appeared to be cheering. Below the detailed, competent drawing was a block of extensive text, written in Hungarian.

Erica looked up, contorting her face. "That doesn't seem too nice."

Chuckling, Patrik pointed to the ancient execution document. "It definitely wasn't nice, but this was a time when the wrong word said to the wrong person...got you dead."

Looking again at the paper, Erica scrunched her face as she tried to decipher the writing. "My Hungarian is bad enough, but this is...."

Reaching over, Patrik pulled the document close. Leaning over it, he focused on the flowing penmanship.

"The writing is an older form of Hungarian. It's difficult, even for a native to read," said Patrik, perusing the passages carefully and mouthing words. "It says: 'The last to be punished for consorting with demons swore vengeance eternal...on those that inherit this land...for not embracing the path to freedom from the Ottoman yoke.'"

Sitting back in her chair, Erica's expression became sober as she mulled over his words. As if to assuage her worries, Patrik offered her a weak smile, one that made neither of them feel better.

"These are fantasies of a bygone and bloody era," Patrik finally said. "But if someone believes this garbage, imagine what they could do. There's plenty of crazy people around."

Erica appeared doubtful as she considered the situation surrounding the recent murders. Speaking slowly, she mulled over Patrik's suggestion of a wayward nutcase. "Whoever is doing this now doesn't have a religious purpose, so it can't be for some ancient reason that people are getting killed. Our only clue is this curse from the 'Order of Vengeance' guy that was executed?"

Hesitant, Patrik shook his head indecisively. He stayed quiet as they peered at each other, both appearing unhappy with the direction of the conversation.

Finally, Erica grew bolder, leaning close and sounding upbeat. "Patrik, you conduct research for a living. I have a simple question."

Raising his eyebrows in response, he focused through his glinting lenses. Sweat beaded on his upper lip, which threatened to release the droplets. "Yes?"

"What if there's truth to this legend, this curse? What if there's something here...we can't understand?"

Patrik scoffed, staring at Erica as if she were joking.

Erica returned his unintentional ridicule with clear eyes. No hint of amusement crossed her features.

"There's something terrible going on," continued Erica, speaking slowly and without reservation. "I can feel it. It isn't normal, and I don't think it has anything to do with the world as we know it."

Taking in her words, Patrik leaned back and shrugged. He smiled innocently, but his eyes became unnerved. "It might not matter for your purposes, Erica, what is happening. Either way, you have something evil to deal with. I would encourage you to be very careful here."

Patrik pushed the gory image in front of Erica again, leaving it in her custody. Breathing in, he made a wiping-clean motion with his hands. "As for me, this is where I'm out of it. I can't be drawn into these events, whether real or imagined. Life is too short, and I'm too feeble."

Working through her confusion, Erica put her finger on the paper, staring intently at the representations of the long-dead Order-of-Vengeance men. The coloring was crude, but the drawing depicted the centuries-old execution with shocking clarity.

Staring over at Patrik, she nodded her understanding.

Collecting her things, Erica pondered the spooky conversation and smiled appreciatively at Patrik. Reflexively, her face grew worried, and she moved her gaze to the nervous group of police standing guard around them.

* * *

The narrow street was rowdy in the late evening. Fuzzy lights illuminated dirty pavement near some dented lampposts, and crowds of revelers flowed through the busy district on personal quests of debauchery and intoxication.

On either side of the street was a hodgepodge of cars parked at odd angles, as if their drivers had decided to annoy as many people as possible with their poor parking skills.

Along the road was an assortment of massage parlors and bars, with an occasional cheap restaurant or liquor store mixed in. Around the various businesses, residents of the neighborhood kept to themselves as they shuffled near heavy traffic and by the occasional bicyclist.

In the distance, music thumped from an unseen nightclub.

Looking out of place, Laszlo stood next to his car, fearful of leaving it alone in the rough neighborhood. Looking down, he engaged the automatic lock with his remote clicker and turned away. His eyes were wary but invigorated as he focused on the sights of the lively district.

As he moved into the busy neighborhood, Laszlo scanned the windows of nearby stores and apartments, reacquainting himself with their visual and audible feel.

Areas like this were gritty, but it was a grit that grew on its citizens. He had always heard that home is in the eye of the beholder, and now, striding through his old haunt, he fully understood that truth in a very pronounced way.

As Laszlo walked toward a distant set of bars, he considered his life: what he needed, as well as what he might want in the future. A word like *happiness* meant different things to different people, but to him, it meant getting and doing what he desired—and having no restraints holding him back from the things he coveted.

Each of his steps matched the upbeat party vibe of this economically poor area. Laszlo's pace picked up, and his mind made him feel at home, as if putting his hand inside a worn but cozy glove. It may have been a nasty and disused glove, but it was nevertheless his, and it was quite comfortable. He trembled with anticipation as he looked ahead.

Moving toward his favorite dive bar, he stopped, suddenly feeling the angst and shame of his past percolating in his conscience. Trying to focus his thoughts, he wrestled with his emotions and commitments, both of which were disjointed and pulled him in different directions.

Breathing deep with uncertainty, he turned abruptly into an alley on his right. This side street was dark and forbidding, but Laszlo walked without fear into the narrow alleyway. He passed someone puking in a corner, then a small flower shop, where he did a double-take to confirm it was actually a real store in such a deprived location.

Shaking his head, Laszlo pressed ahead, where he turned again into a shadowy tattoo parlor tucked to the side. Above its dingy entrance, the establishment's lovely name, *Mary's Bitch*, was painted in a garish red.

Walking inside, the door opened with a jingle of a bell. It was a small place, and a three-hundred-pound tattooist and an enormous customer filling the interior made it tighter still.

Wearing a wife-beater and sweatpants, the brawny tattooist didn't appear to be anyone's bitch, but one could never be sure of such things.

Oleg glanced up from his tattoo work on a fat man lying below him. Sprawled on his stomach, the enormous customer had a half-completed dragon tattoo etched across the folds of his back. Between Oleg's girth and his corpulent client, it looked a bit like they were two tattooed walruses hovering over a tawdry massage bench.

Looking up, Oleg was surprised to see Laszlo. Tilting his head, he turned off his buzzing tattoo gun.

The white jiggly flesh below him bled prodigiously from a dark line he had been tracing with the tool, and Oleg absently wiped blood away from his work. Below, the customer flipped his head to join the stare at Laszlo.

"Laszlo...never thought I'd see you again," Oleg said, his eyes growing confused. "Does Zoltan know you're around?"

Laszlo shifted his weight self-consciously, trying to appear normal, as normal as he could while looking at two sweaty, half-clothed fat men in a dark room.

"Yeah, I was hoping to see him again. It's pretty important; I'm hoping he can help me out," Laszlo admitted, looking ashamed. "Life isn't too great right now."

"I heard about your problems on the news," said Oleg, managing to look empathetic. "Sorry to hear about that. Zoltan should be at his bar. But be careful there. Sometimes you have to know your limits."

The fat man below him nodded his agreement, looking like a sideways Buddha on the table.

Going quiet, Oleg shrugged and restarted the tattoo gun. Getting back to work, he focused fully on his dragon-tattoo creation.

For a fascinating second, Laszlo watched, mesmerized by the bizarre scene, unable to pull his eyes away.

Without saying goodbye, Laszlo turned and exited, retracing his steps out of the shabby business.

Outside, he stopped again in front of the neon-lit bars, where he collected himself. Licking his lips, he panned his gaze about, regretting what was to happen next but knowing he really couldn't turn back.

Making his decision, Laszlo walked to the right and entered a place simply marked *Bar*. With a white-stucco exterior that was neither flashy nor overly descriptive, the name was chosen for function and succinctness rather than flair.

Inside, the lights and atmosphere quickly made him feel nostalgic. In the background, a Hungarian heavy metal band played, belting out indecipherable lyrics.

The tables and chairs in the establishment were relatively clean, and only a few customers sat scattered around the poorly lit room.

Sidling up next to an old man at the bar, Laszlo sat and motioned to the bartender. The sour-faced geezer next to him showed no interest in conversation, preferring a cheap glass of sudsy swill over new company.

The bartender wasn't someone Laszlo knew, which was probably a good thing. The dour man set a coaster in front of Laszlo and gestured to an assortment of bottles lining the lit wall behind him. "What'll it be?"

Unsure of himself, Laszlo hesitated before responding. Coming to a decision, he held up three fingers to indicate the level of pour and stuttered a response, "Whiskey, straight."

Laszlo was rewarded with a quick delivery of his drink of choice. The bartender then turned away, assuming a disinterested scan of the rest of the bar.

Left alone with his drink, Laszlo stared down, captivated by the booze's beautiful golden color. It was rather weird for a simple liquid to be so attractive, but here he was, marveling at a dirty glass in a not-so-dirty bar in a place he probably shouldn't have been.

He smiled at the absurdity of it all. Life was about avoiding the things you enjoy, while also feeling ashamed about it. It was damn depressing. Meanwhile, those with the fortitude to grab what they wanted could live life to the fullest, setting aside their onerous shackles of self-imposed limitations.

Just as important was how those people were perceived. Alpha males ran the companies, got the girls—usually more than one—and everyone respected them without reservation. The weak and humble got left behind, scrambling for scraps and deluding themselves with notions of virtue.

Tentatively, Laszlo reached for the glass.

And the meek shall inherit the Earth.

The voice in Laszlo's head almost made him jump, and he jerked his hand back from the drink. It sounded like Erica, but he knew better than attributing his inner monologue to his ex. She undoubtedly believed such thoughts, but the source of his interior discussions was all about his own self-doubts and conscience. *Probably.*

Laszlo suddenly wished all those catechism classes of his youth were long forgotten, buried in distant times with quaint concepts like sin and redemption. Why was it that he could remember the Virgin Mary statue at church as a boy, but not more than a handful of elements from the periodic table? At least by knowing those elements, he might have landed a better job than selling insurance.

Because truth is eternal, and gratification is temporary.

Laszlo chuckled, shaking his head at his mind's own amateurish philosophical gibberish. It was time to make his own way, to seize the day—or at least the moment.

He reached again for the glass, but as he extended his fingers, a large hand fell on his shoulder. The grip from vice-like fingers made him wince, and staring back, his eyes locked with Zoltan's.

Zoltan was a bear of a man, and not the cuddly kind. Tall and broad, he looked like he could easily play for the New York Jets, with the stipulation that the team might actually win if he did so. His tangled beard was vast and dense, spilling down his chest and looking like it could house a nest of birds.

Zoltan's angry eyes focused down on Laszlo, narrowing as his grip tightened. "What are you doing here, Laszlo? Do you remember the part I told you before, where I said you are never to set foot here again?"

Grimacing, Laszlo set the drink down. Ashamed, he nodded up at Zoltan with an apologetic frown. "Yeah, but I need your help. The kind only you can provide."

* * *

The outline of Parliament stretched along the northern Danube River, creating a dark silhouette against the sparkling stars. On the east side of the river, the structure lay between two bridges crossing over the opposite sides of the sprawling capital.

The elaborate building was the seat of the Hungarian government, and it looked the part. Massive stone blocks, chiseled to perfection, were sculpted with late-nineteenth-century Gothic influence, creating a monumental impression. Rows of lights adorned the top of a series of black spires, and a central dome served as a striking centerpiece to the wide complex.

At the time of its construction, Hungary was much larger, and such an imposing building was once necessary to govern vast territories under the Austro-Hungarian Empire. Now that its administrative reach had been reduced by the tides of history, the building seemed almost as lonely as it was beautiful.

Large portions of the castle-like structure were now dark and unused, but it still functioned as the center of governance. One of the most visited sites in the city, it was immaculately maintained. Clusters of specialist workers ensured the upkeep of the building and grounds, while custodians and their cleaning vehicles kept the exterior walls and walkways spotless.

Around the building's stone exterior were groups of police and military, billeted to ensure the safety of tourists and government officials. Even at this time of night, or perhaps especially during that time period, there was a significant presence of protective officers to watch over it.

Three policemen currently stood in front of the building, looking bored as they faced the river.

Tibor Papp shook his head, gesturing at the well-lit area around them. Tibor was well-built, but he hunched in a way that gave him a stooped appearance, as if his shoulders were too far back for his frame.

Tibor's whiny voice pierced the silence of the calm evening. "How long are they gonna keep us on twelve-hour shifts? This boring shit is killing me."

His companions, Istvan and Zoli, chuckled. They were also police officers, but unlike Tibor, they seemed to enjoy their work.

"Well, the pay is good, anyway. If this keeps up, I'll have enough to get that SUV," said Istvan, beaming at the thought of bigger a paycheck.

Zoli chuckled, speaking in a mocking tone. "Right, great idea. There's a lot better ways to get a car than working yourself to death. Why drive a vehicle that takes two years of pay to buy, then half your monthly cash to maintain and gas it up? I see why you became a cop instead of a financial guru."

Istvan feigned offense, then lowered his voice and gestured to Zoli. "Ah, right. It's a much better plan to give half your money every month to your ex and only see your kids every other week? All because you left her for a twenty-year-old."

"Really, twenty?" said Tibor, now intrigued enough to join the conversation. "I'm impressed, Zoli—for once. Wow."

Zoli didn't respond, avoiding both of their gazes. Chewing on his lip, he regarded his colleagues with an acid stare, like he was hoping they would suddenly keel over.

Istvan continued, his smile widening. "Yeah, but the problem is, someone caught his new girlfriend screwing the captain on the night shift at the City Park. They shined their lights on his white pumping ass, on duty, while Zoli's new girl was taking one for the team. Apparently, Zoli's homewrecker liked to have more than just one cop as a sugar daddy. God, I wish I'd seen that."

Tibor and Istvan burst out laughing. Istvan laughed so hard, his breaths growing short from the effort, that tears eventually ran down his face. As the cackling continued, Zoli merely stood, shaking his head and gnawing on his lip.

"That's some cold shit, guys. Kicking a man while he's down," Zoli responded. "There'll come a day when you need my help, and I'm gonna remind you of this boring-ass night at Parliament. You'll see. It'll be payback time."

As the chuckles died away, Tibor nodded, blinking away his amusement.

"Speaking of cars, they took me off patrol to babysit this place," Tibor said, motioning to the half-dark Parliament. "I hate doing guard duty."

Zoli shook his head, looking at Tibor like he had a screw loose. "I could never figure out why you like writing tickets all day. Traffic is the worst duty on the force, by far."

"Yeah," added Istvan. "We could spend our time here, looking at hot German tourists...or, we could write tickets to rich old men. It doesn't take a genius to figure out the better option."

Tibor raised his arm, mimicking a talking hand. "Blah blah blah. If you guys wanted to stay security guards, you could go back to the mall. Honestly, that'd be a better use of your law enforcement talents. Or lack of them."

Tibor pointed south, where the Chain Bridge spanned the Danube. The old-style suspension bridge passed over the pedestrian walkway, hugging the river's shoreline underneath its span.

The bridge itself extended into a mist that roiled over the flowing water. Though lit by extensive lampposts, the fog reduced visibility along that part of the river.

"I'm going to check out the walkway," said Tibor. "Maybe I'll meet some interesting people to pass the time with. People worth talking to, for once."

Tibor paced away from his companions, trudging toward the looming bridge structure in the drizzly night. As he moved deeper into the gloom, his form melted into the haze.

Zoli grinned as Tibor's silhouette faded down the path, but abruptly, his smile wilted. Gesturing after Tibor, he raised his voice, a frown crossing his face. "Um, the sergeant said we had to do all foot patrols together until they find this psycho."

Nodding, Istvan stumbled after Tibor. As he picked up the pace, his boots squeaked against the empty riverwalk. "Ah, yeah, let's catch up to him."

Hurrying down the pathway, with the mist thickening, Zoli called out, "Tibor, wait up!"

Irritated, Tibor pressed ahead, ignoring his companions. Stopping under the bridge, he placed his elbows on the railing, looking out over the gentle, churning water of the Danube. Brooding, he took in the impressive sight, even with the reduced visibility.

Above, three quick jabbing shadows flitted from underneath the bridge. Tibor convulsed from the unexpected attack. Not knowing what had happened, he raised his hand to feel his head. His fingers were suddenly covered in blood, so much that it appeared he had dipped them in a bucket of gore.

Hustling toward Tibor, Istvan peered into the shadows, alarmed and trying to figure out what had just happened. His eyes widened as he glanced over at Zoli.

"What the fuck?" Istvan shouted.

Already drawing his pistol, Zoli yelled out to their friend, "Tibor, we're coming!"

With his own pistol now in hand, Istvan keyed his radio. Panic filled his voice as he shouted into the receiver. "Officer down. Chain Bridge, east side—underneath the span over the walkway. We're engaging the suspect."

His head lulling, Tibor tried responding to Zoli, but only a nonsensical gurgle escaped his lips. Blood gushed from open wounds on the top of his head, shoulder, and neck. Facing his incoming friends, he dropped to his knees, just managing to avoid toppling over.

From behind, a dark hand grabbed his hair, yanking his head back. The Huntsman's wicked blade slowly lowered toward Tibor's unprotected neck.

* * *

Janos stood on the roof of Parliament, relaxing and looking over the mist-shrouded river below. Despite the late hour, he was wide awake, and the brisk night air kept his attention clear and mood upbeat.

Life was good as a cop, and in fact, it couldn't have been better. He had the best job in the city, and almost nobody knew anything about it.

Who would have thought they would pay him so much to do what he loved: nothing? Grinning to himself, he popped a piece of gum into his mouth, smacking in grand fashion.

Lowering night vision goggles over his eyes, he scanned the river path that passed in front of Parliament. Staring intently, he took in the view slowly, carefully watching each person who was out at such a late hour.

A few couples walked hand in hand to the north, sharing a dark stroll with no crowds or sounds to bother them. If Janos was a romantic guy, which he was decidedly not, it would have offered the perfect backdrop for an affectionate interaction.

Next, his gaze fell on a strange guy dressed in a toga walking toward a deserted platform that abutted the dark current at the river's edge. The stumbling drunk carried a large easel, and he appeared to be searching for a place to set up and create his masterwork painting.

Janos shook his head with a grin. *Only in Budapest.*

Casting his barely chewed gum aside, he extracted a cigarette from a pack in his web gear. Flipping open his Zippo lighter, he leaned down and lit it. Sucking in the noxious fumes, he nodded contentedly. *Best duty on the force.*

The radio in his earpiece chirped:

"Officer down. Chain Bridge, east side—underneath the span over the walkway. We're engaging the suspect."

Shocked, Janos flipped down his goggles and scanned south near the Chain Bridge. There, he saw a large and bizarre-looking man drop from the girders underneath the bridge. Hunched on his knees near the man was a cop, barely able to hold himself upright.

Oh shit, oh shit, oh shit. Terrified, Janos tossed his cigarette aside and sprawled on the roof. Reaching to the side, he snatched his Springfield rifle, quickly pulling it close and resting his cheek on the stock. Squinting, he peered through the scope, panning to take in the crazy scene below.

Searching through the optic for his target, Janos quickly located the cop and zoomed in on the grievously wounded man. With a face covered in blood and looking half-dead, the poor guy balanced on his knees, quivering while he awaited his fate.

The Huntsman grasped the cop's hair and lowered a blade to his neck, preparing to administer a savage cut. This coup de grâce, delivered by some maniac with a black blade, wasn't going to be pretty.

Gulping, Janos focused his reticle on the attacker's chest. *Please God, let me get this right.*

Pulling the trigger, his .30 caliber rifle bucked in his hands, recoiling with a sharp *CRACK*. Racking the bolt, he fired again, his expert motions making the shots quick and precise.

* * *

Getting in range of the assailant, Istvan got into a firing stance and aimed down his barrel. Keeping his night sights squarely on the dark shape, he hesitated, unsure of whether to fire.

He's too close; I'll hit Tibor.

Pulling up next to Istvan, Zoli also focused on his own pistol's sights. Neither appeared eager to risk hitting their friend. While Tibor balanced on his knees, the moment became strangely silent.

Carefully, the Huntsman held Tibor by the hair and brought the black dagger to his throat. Unafraid, the attacker prepared to end his life.

The crack of a rifle split the night, and the Huntsman recoiled from a supersonic bullet striking his chest. Releasing his grip on Tibor, the hulking assailant stepped back, raising his head to look toward the top of the distant parliament building.

Released from his impending execution, Tibor slumped to the ground, his head smacking the pavement.

But the Huntsman didn't appear bothered. Another shot boomed from a distant rifle, and he flinched again, struck by another deadly projectile.

Still, he didn't fall from the deadly impacts. He barely seemed injured, despite what should have been devastating sniper shots.

Taking their cue, Zoli and Istvan opened fire, pulling their triggers as fast as their fingers allowed. A hail of bullets struck the vicious stranger, sending the Huntsman stumbling back under the barrage of gunfire.

Retreating a few steps, the Huntsman hesitated as bullets riddled his body. Crouching, he jumped straight up, grabbing a metal bar under the bridge and pulling himself into the darkness. Now out of sight, his form had disappeared, lost in the shadows of the bridge's extensive rigging.

Running up to his crumpled friend, Istvan reached down to Tibor's unmoving body. His fearful eyes focused on the bloody man as he ran his hands over Tibor's head and face, ignoring the copious blood as he searched for a pulse.

Stunned, Istvan stopped, slowly pulling away from their fallen friend and sadly bowing his head.

Peering up, he met Zoli's distressed gaze. Shaking his head, fear and grief filled his expression.

* * *

On top of Parliament, Janos struggled to reacquire the target. Panning the rifle back and forth, he scanned frantically, searching through the shadows. *Where did you go?*

A loud alarm split the night. Sirens wailed from somewhere on the dark perimeter of the massive building complex. Flashing emergency lights erupted from multiple directions as police vehicles and special response units awakened to the sudden violence.

Janos' earpiece echoed with a flood of questions, stern voices demanding to know what was happening, who was shooting—*and what the hell was being shot at?*

In response, he stammered, barely relaying the information over the radio, describing both the events and a description of the bizarre perpetrator. Trying to stay calm, he spoke with shrill words, forcing his cracking voice to relay what was happening.

From higher on the bridge, Janos suddenly saw his target reemerge. The odd figure ran in great leaps across the sloping supports of the suspension towers.

Constructed to allow for easy access to maintenance areas atop the bridge, the Huntsman was able to sprint atop this slick, dangerous pathway with no regard for his safety. Bounding ahead in an almost mechanical manner, his outline was clear and recognizable.

With enough speed and courage, any person could cross the whole bridge without touching the

126

pedestrian or street portions of the span. Apparently this lunatic had both of those qualities in abundance.

Breathing carefully, Janos led the Huntsman ever so slightly through his scope. Just before the figure disappeared into the mist atop the supports, Janos pulled the trigger.

His rifle cracked again. The strange assailant convulsed from the impact of the bullet, then vanished into the fog.

Trying to control his disbelief, Janos shouted into his radio, "Attacker...engaged. I hit 'em, I think. He's fleeing across the Chain Bridge to the Buda side. He's...running on top of the tower supports."

Chapter Seven

Standing near the kitchen table, Erica stared through the window, her frown heavy with dismay. She licked her lips, dread and trepidation etched in her worried expression.

Behind her, Monica sat in the living room, staring at the TV with a similar look of desperation and anxiety.

In shock, Erica collected herself and turned to watch television, where a chaotic scene was playing out on the news report.

Erica was aghast at the situation, the deaths, the uncertainty, and her own prospects for the future. Regret and worry had always been part of her life, but this new and terrifying chapter of fear and abject murder was overwhelming.

The thought that this ongoing violence and craziness might also affect her precious daughter added another horrific layer to her struggle to build a life in this new country. She always seen herself as a practical person, but what was now happening seemed to defy any effort at understanding.

Stunned, Erica wondered if things would ever get better, or if the constant anxiety that had lodged in her mind over the last few years was here to stay. Heartbreak and divorce had already taken a toll on her personal world, but now something far worse had crept into her life.

Brooding, she thought about the wider context of these horrifying events. And as if her taste buds decided to rebel at their current circumstance, an acrid taste filled her dry mouth. Trying to drive away the revolting taste, she smacked her lip several times.

Truth was, it had only been a few generations since the Holocaust and war devastated the long-suffering Hungarian people, and this ordeal was soon followed by forty-five years of Soviet repression, mass deportations, and even a brief revolution.

This recent murderous psychopath and his crimes were minor in comparison to that horrible past, but that historical perspective seemed quaint when it was your own family that could be the next victim to whatever was happening. In fact, it was Stalin who once said, "The death of one man is a tragedy; the death of millions is a statistic."

That evil bastard would certainly have known that, but the cruel truth was, when you worried about your child, you would trade the grief of the entire world to protect your own from harm. Of course, Erica realized this was a selfish perspective, but one that was true across all times and cultures. Considering whether she would trade a thousand lives for Monica's safety, she quickly came to an internal answer that left her with no sense of personal virtue.

On the television, various announcers spoke engagingly about the killing of cop Tibor Papp, as if taking turns to sound the most sorrowful about his death. Accompanying their somber voices, a

Hungarian flag fluttered in the corner of the TV screen as a small tribute to his passing.

Erica let her mind wander to thoughts about the poor deceased policeman. Die of a heart attack, and a person might become a footnote in history, but if he dies violently at the hands of a criminal, everyone wanted to mourn him in the strongest possible manner.

She suspected the cop's family would find little comfort in such public accolades, but at least it was a kind gesture to be fondly remembered by society.

Outside, sirens brayed through the night. Police vehicles raced through the streets below, their wails blending with the chaos surrounding the Castle District.

Far below, on the river, two helicopters hovered over the water, casting search lights up and down the waterway. The outlines of their bright searchlight cones stabbed into the dissipating fog as they hunted for the murderous aggressor.

"It almost sounds like an air raid," Erica said, moving to the window and peering down. Rising onto her toes, she strained to see farther down the street. "In fact, that has to be what the sirens are for. Not a sound I ever thought I'd hear."

"Mom, they're still looking for the bad man," Monica replied, her bulging, frightened eyes pivoting away from the TV. "He attacked a policeman."

Erica moved near the TV, where she watched the images that had been playing since the attack happened. Scowling at the incessantly bad information, she lowered the volume with the remote.

Thinking of her daughter, she paced to the couch, leaned down, and hugged her. Monica's anxious eyes held back tears as she clutched her mother.

"They'll find whoever is doing this, Mon," Erica said, though her own eyes appeared unconvinced at such a possibility. "Nobody can get away with something like this."

A sharp knock at the door startled her. Dreading a visitor, Erica glanced out the window. Four police officers stood down there in the building's alcove, each holding a shotgun and carefully watching pedestrians who walked by the building.

Laszlo's voice called out from the other side of the apartment's front door, his tone a mix of pleading and determination. "Erica, open up, please. All hell is breaking loose out here."

Hurrying to the door, Erica swung it wide. Laszlo stood in the hallway, flanked by two serious-faced officers, men who appeared equally as upset as her ex-husband.

Laszlo appeared afraid, but there was also a motivated and firm look to his countenance. Erica had never thought of Laszlo as courageous, in fact nobody did, but now a bit of that unaccustomed trait flashed across his face.

"I can't sit at home anymore," said Laszlo, his eyes darting between Erica and Monica. "Can I come in?"

* * *

Laszlo sat still on the couch, his features locked in confusion. On the coffee table to his front was a glass of iced tea, and to his side was his daughter.

Leaning against his shoulder, Monica's eyes were puffy and red. Various levels of anxiety, fear, and sadness filled her expression. Her family's precarious physical security undoubtedly played a large role in her current emotional weakness, but the death of at least one of her teachers probably didn't help her ongoing trauma.

Truthfully, though, Monica wasn't as sad as might be expected for her circumstance. When someone you knew and didn't like died, even as a young person, tears could be difficult to arrange, at least in flowing abundance. *No harm in admitting that*, Monica thought. *In fact, they were the worst adults I've ever known.*

Erica paced across the room, her eyes darting from the floor to the windows in a manic rhythm. Back and forth she marched, punctuating each turn on the carpet with a perplexed frown.

If not for the police lights outside illuminating her determined face, she might have looked like a mad professor pondering some unsolvable math theorem. Problem was, her family's current situation needed a solution rather quickly, and the fact that her math skills stopped at the times tables made a near-term answer to their problems unlikely.

"There has to be something we can do," Erica said, her voice low and flustered. "How is any of this happening? I never even knew anyone killed in an accident, and now we got a serial killer on the loose, wiping people out. Normal people shouldn't have to go through this."

"I doubt we can do more than the police," replied Laszlo, still looking confused. "I think they're going to have plenty of motivation to solve this now. There's a big difference between somebody hurting street people and attacking cops on duty."

Laszlo glanced up at Erica. He was suddenly bashful, offering her a self-conscious, pained smile. His awkward grin became almost boyish. "How are you doing?"

Erica pursed her lips, taking in their surroundings with a wide gesture of her arms. "Other than being trapped in this place by a madman, things are just peachy. Are you trying to ask the dumbest questions possible?"

From Laszlo's side, Monica glared up at her mom. Her disapproving frown stopped Erica's attempt at bitchiness in its tracks.

Finding her patience, Erica took a deep breath and softened her voice. She also did a passable job of sounding like she cared about her next question. "How are you, Laszlo? How is your friend—Natalia?"

Laszlo dropped his eyes to his tea, a reluctant smile crossing his lips. Sitting up, he pulled the glass close and twirled it on the coaster.

"Haven't heard a word from her," Laszlo explained, managing to appear both hurt and deserving of sympathy. "She's not answering my calls. Guess I deserve that—with everything that's happened."

He took a sip of his drink, letting the sweet liquid swirl in his mouth as he considered his next question. "What about you? Have you met...someone?"

Erica calmed herself before giving an honest answer. "Well, I thought I had something going on. I met a real good guy. But I don't know what will happen now. I think he ran for the hills, and I don't blame him. Rampaging killers have a way of dampening romance."

Laszlo nodded and chuckled. Opening his mouth to speak, he thought better of it and went silent.

Next to Laszlo, Monica pulled her head off his shoulder and stared at her mom. "Mom, when are you and Dad getting back together? I'm getting sick of living in different places."

Taken by surprise, Erica's face flushed. Looking like a deer caught in particularly bright-bulbed headlights, she stumbled over her words. "Well, Mon, I...um...we are divorced now. Sometimes adults have to live in different places."

Thankfully, Laszlo came to her rescue. Leaning near Monica, he tried to sound cheerful. "Mommy has a new...friend, sweetie. Don't worry, I'll always be around, and you can come over whenever you want."

Doubtful, Monica straightened and fixed an aggressive gaze on her mother. Her nostrils flared, and her face grew cold as she spoke. "I don't want to come over. I want to be a family again. This visiting stuff is stupid. Dad belongs here. We're a family."

Laszlo looked like he didn't disagree with the sentiment, but Erica shook her head forcefully. She kept shaking it, even as Monica was getting more wound up.

Monica's eyes turned angry, almost hateful, and she focused entirely on Erica. Her demeanor took on the appearance of a Mafia boss making Erica an offer she simply couldn't refuse.

"I don't want Adam around," Monica said, her tone rising. "He's not my dad."

Laszlo didn't know what to do or say, so he opted for an apologetic, groveling stare at his ex-wife. This quiet approach to problem-solving, being a tried-and-true method of avoiding spousal rage—even from an ex-spouse—kept him out of trouble for the moment. Erica ignored him.

Erica became quiet, glancing at the prints on the wall as she considered her daughter's veto power over her dating life. Not even Sammy Davis Jr. had an answer for her.

"Mon, we've been through this before. This is how it has to be from now on," Erica said, trying to be firm. "Sometimes we can't change what's happened in life."

Erica then gave an annoyed glance at the cowering Laszlo, who looked like he wanted the killer to burst in and interrupt, hoping for anything to improve the deteriorating discussion.

Standing abruptly, Monica shot Erica a pissed-off glare and stormed off to her room.

Frustrated, Erica watched her go without a word. Brooding for several quiet moments, she nervously rubbed her knuckles.

More awkward silence continued. Finally, Laszlo broke the quiet, sounding conciliatory and gesturing to himself. "I'm sorry for all this. We both know it's all my fault, but I have a favor to ask: Would you mind if I stay over and sleep on the couch?"

He nodded back toward Monica's room, where a thump accompanied something being thrown against the door.

Frowning, Laszlo looked down, trying to appear brave. Contrasting with his sour expression, his tone grew upbeat, and he managed to sound convincing. "I'm not leaving her alone till this is all over. For once, I'm going to be here when she needs me."

* * *

The cavernous police office was laid out with multiple rows of desks. Collections of filing cabinets blocked off portions of the huge room, allowing for sections of specialized departments throughout the cluttered environment to have some physical separation.

Rows of lamps recessed in the ceiling cast a bright light on the assembled workspaces below. Workers peered at their monitors, squinting at their screens under the glowing light. The arrangement ensured sufficient illumination for people to do their jobs, and a beneficial side effect of the abundant lighting was that nobody could nod off in the bright environment.

The chattering of radios was loud, sounding something like a cramped version of NASA's mission control. Officers in uniform and detectives in plain clothes rushed back and forth, carrying out various administrative tasks.

Nemeth stood in the corner of the expansive room, away from most of the ruckus. Frustrated, he faced an enormous map of Budapest, staring at colored pins denoting assorted units throughout the metropolis.

Sighing, he rubbed his tired eyes, trying to overcome a lack of sleep.

The radio on his crowded desk blared an announcement, the dispatcher sounding hurried and excited.

"Please be advised, the suspect has been spotted entering the front entrance of the Gellért Baths. Wildcat One, move to the target and neutralize as necessary. Wildcats Two and Three move to backup and provide support. Ensure civilians are protected at all times."

Nemeth stared at the radio for several moments longer, as if doing so would encourage more information to emerge. But nothing came, and he mulled over the situation with a disappointed nod.

Turning back to the map, Nemeth studied the city in its entirety. Looking serious, his eyes grew detached as he thought through his options.

"Sergeant, where are the Special Response Teams we discussed?" Nemeth asked, tracing over several streets with his finger as he considered the approaches to the ancient Gellért Bathhouse. "Can't anyone move the process along?"

Shuffling papers on a nearby desk, Sergeant Kovacs smacked his lips and nodded enthusiastically. He was near Nemeth's age, but his pale face had largely managed to avoid Nemeth's frown lines and dark circles.

Standing, Kovacs gestured to the map. "They're on their way from District Eleven. Three total. It took a while to get them approved by the Defense Ministry, but the latest attack seems to have lit a fire under their asses."

Nodding, Nemeth turned and met Kovacs' gaze. His voice was incredulous, as if he were repeating something absurd that he knew to be true. "Good. Reports are that the subject is well protected by body armor. He's been shot numerous times, with...no obvious effect."

Nemeth turned back to the map, planting his hands on his hips as he appraised the entire area. Moving up, he planted a lone black pin on a spot on the west side of the river. "Have one of the teams deploy to the Gellért Baths. The others are to stay in reserve, ready for anything this lunatic might do. Make sure they remain mobile at all times."

Kovacs nodded, looking serious and resolute. Thinking for a moment, he snapped a finger, having remembered something.

Rummaging through some paperwork on his desk, Kovacs pulled out a photo. Moving near Nemeth, he gently set the color picture on the desk, handling it like it required particular care.

Kovacs peered up with an anxious frown, his eyes full of sadness. "This came in a few minutes ago, from a site exactly fifty-eight kilometers downstream from Margaret Island. Add another victim to the death toll."

The picture was of Markita Horvath, the wife of the murdered schoolteacher Andreas Horvath. Her clothes were tattered and muddy, and she was pale, waterlogged, and unmistakably dead.

She lay on a nameless dirt beach on some remote stretch of the Danube River. Her death pose wasn't a good look for her, and her unseeing eyes seemed to drift to the side, as if she were unwilling to meet the gaze of the photographer.

Rubbing his hands over his face, Nemeth pressed his palms against his eyes, wishing he could unsee the image. Fatigued with all the drama and violence, he also wished someone else was overseeing this clusterfuck investigation.

For that matter, he wished his vacation to Albania next month could be moved up. After all, the Adriatic Sea was a wonderful place to visit at this time of year, and there seemed to be fewer homicidal killers there.

Sighing, Nemeth muttered under his breath, "Great. Another body."

* * *

The siren wailed from atop the dark police van, its spinning lights announcing its emergency purpose. Banking through cramped streets, the special police vehicle seemed too large for its surroundings, yet it didn't slow down.

To the front of the veering van, rows of mismatched cars pulled out of the way as the police vehicle made sharp turns through intersections and around clusters of parked autos.

Inside, five hardened SWAT members sat across from each other on metal benches. As the vehicle sped along, each man held magazines in his grip, feeding loose 9mm ammunition into them.

Hanging at each of their sides were MP-5 submachine guns, and on the rest of their web gear were all manner of lights and support equipment. On their heads were clean military helmets with night-vision goggles attached.

There was a steely determination in the men, but also worry, the kind of concentrated worry that comes from officers who made their living preparing for violence. Their precise eye movements were focused on their tasks, as they avoided anxiety by focusing on their gear and responsibilities.

After finishing topping off the last of his magazines, the SWAT leader tapped it against his helmet and slammed it into his weapon. Racking the bolt forward, he nodded to the rest of the men. They followed suit by checking and rechecking each other's equipment and loadouts.

For several moments, they continued to ensure functionality and proper storage of lights, tools, and flash grenades. Satisfied, the serious-eyed men sat back, signaling with a nod they were ready for whatever came next.

Leaning close to his radio, the commander keyed it with his thumb. His voice was smooth and professional. "Command, this is Wildcat One. ETA three minutes. Will hold COMMS and inform as we proceed to the target. Over."

Listening to a reply, the SWAT leader then twirled his finger in a circle to confirm the mission was ready. His men nodded in response, preparing for what was next.

Looking toward the rear-entry door of the vehicle, the commander waited for their arrival at the target. Though appearing professional, the wary anticipation of what came next stood out in his expectant expression.

* * *

The Gellért Baths stood alone in the nighttime surroundings, facing a major intersection. Not in a residential area, the building was devoid of pedestrians or customers at this late hour.

The dated front of the worn complex was constructed of old bricks and weathered stone columns. Above the entrance, the words HOTEL GELLERT GYOGYSZALLO were chiseled into its timeworn facade.

The Wildcat One SWAT van careened into the parking area and screeched to a stop in front of the antique structure. Its five members piled out the back door, moving carefully toward the front of the building as they scanned their surroundings.

The officers' eyes carefully swept the vicinity as they approached, with each man peering through night-vision goggles to scour the area more clearly. Professional and vigilant, every step they made was practiced and deliberate, every movement smooth.

Behind them, two more vans pulled into blocking positions at either end of the street fronting the baths. With doors swinging open, groups of other special policemen disgorged under the streetlights, rushing to take up positions in support of the main assault force.

Farther away, several regular police cars stopped and blocked roads within close distance to the building. From these vehicles, officers hurriedly set up cones across traffic and directed people away from the developing scene, keeping potential drivers or gawkers from approaching.

The primary assault group approached cautiously, their weapon lights scanning windows and doors as they got closer. On the second floor, above the entrance, a broken window provided sufficient access for a large man to get inside. Their flashlights circled over the jagged hole as they assessed the potential entry point of the fleeing killer.

The SWAT leader stepped to the side of the wooden entry door and motioned to one of his men. The man rushed forward with a small sledgehammer. Holding it back, he bashed the door several times. The doorframe shuddered under the blows before bursting inward.

"Going in," the leader whispered into his mic.

The door hung by one hinge, revealing the unlit space beyond. Casting the hammer aside, the breeching officer motioned for the other cops to move in, and the team crept into the darkness beyond.

Inside, the members spread out, their necks swiveling as their lights stabbed into the dark corners of the seemingly deserted building. Stepping carefully, they moved quietly, scanning the area through their optics.

Around them, more stone columns flanked the path down a long-tiled hallway. Their lights illuminated patches of the public-facing interior, showing painted walls depicting Roman villas and cheerful images of smiling families.

By day, the artwork would undoubtedly have been appealing, but in the patchy light, coupled with padding of footfalls across the hard floor, it appeared forbidding.

Moving forward, the team's beams crisscrossed the darkness, probing for prospective threats. Finding none, the men crept farther down the hall.

At the end of the extended hallway, a large pool lay undisturbed. Its placid surface reflected their lights, casting eerie illumination across the far wall. The shimmering effect made the water seem otherworldly and mysterious.

The pool itself was on the first floor, but above it was another level that created an open-air space over the water. This elevated area allowed a vantage point to watch swimming and relaxation below, providing a cozy backdrop for entertainment and lounging swimmers during business hours.

To the side, a single set of dark marble steps led to the next floor.

Creeping into the pool area, the team leader gestured up the stairs with three fingers, while he and one of the other men moved to search the ground floor at the same time. Without hesitation, three of the police operators detached and hurried up the steps.

When the first cop reached the top, there was a *THUNK*, and the man stumbled, his body going limp. A dark spearhead was half-emerged from the back of his head, and he crumpled backward, dead before he even hit the steps.

As the corpse landed on his back, the point of the protruding weapon caught on a step as he slid down, causing a weird scraping sound as bits of his brain leaked onto the hard marble steps.

The next teammate began to fire, spraying bullets into the darkness even before he crested the staircase above his dead companion.

The Huntsman stood in the darkness, not far from the top of the stairs, his dark silhouette waiting for them. Moving worryingly fast, his brutish shape lurched toward the officers.

The men blasted their weapons at the emerging shadow, and flashes of their erupting gunfire lit the shadowy area. Being so close to their target, there was simply no way they could miss the huge figure.

But there was no apparent effect from their bullets. The clinking of projectiles striking the Huntsman's body were loud, like high-pitched pebbles ricocheting off a metal shield. But the hooded Huntsman advanced, reaching out toward the remaining two men as their eyes went wide.

Seizing the weapon of one cop, the Huntsman picked him up by his attached strap and threw him off the staircase. The flailing man crashed into the water below, splashing into the smooth surface as he pinwheeled his arms. Trying to right himself but weighed down by his gear, he surged his arms, clutching at the water and struggling to stay afloat.

Below and near the pool, the shocked SWAT leader looked up. Pivoting toward the stairs, he sprinted to reinforce his men, moving with urgent lunges to help his team members.

Coming to the bottom of the stairs, he stared up, his frantic eyes focusing on the second floor's landing. There he saw the Huntsman, who held another man off the ground in an iron grip.

With ruthless speed, the vicious Huntsman plunged a dark dagger into his captive's back, ramming the blade all the way through his torso. The splitting sound of the man's guts being exposed accompanied his anguished screams.

Blood splashed from the horrific wound, and the Huntsman held the man tight, then cast the struggling body down the steps. The eviscerated man landed on the marble with a wet thump, sliding down the steps as his body convulsed and spasmed.

The Huntsman, his shadowed face hidden in the cowl of his strange hood, now stared down at the SWAT leader.

Behind the leader, the last cop moved up to help. The man, shorter than the leader, had wide eyes as he aimed his weapon up the stairs.

"Shit, shoot him in the head," shouted the leader.

Panicked, the officers opened fire, the flashes of their guns breaking the darkness.

The blasts of gunfire struck the Huntsman in the face, his head recoiling from the impacts. Subsequent bursts of gunfire struck again and again, and his head convulsed with each whizzing bullet.

But the Huntsman did not fall. Recoiling from the shots, the monster merely shrugged off what should have been mortal wounds. There seemed to be no effect, with the bullets pinging harmlessly into the darkness.

With his weapon clicking empty, the leader let his gun swing free and raised his angry face to the Huntsman.

"Die, you fuck," he shouted, unsheathing a long combat knife. Drawing a deep breath, he charged up the stairs, bounding two steps at a time toward their enormous adversary.

The Huntsman's arm shot out, grabbing the SWAT leader by the throat. With shocking ease, he lifted the policeman from the stairs and batted the knife from his hand.

Turning his head, the Huntsman's dark-hooded face looked down at the last man in the fight. While the leader flailed uselessly, the Huntsman tilted his head at the remaining cop at the bottom of the stairs, as if curious what he planned to do.

The last officer had had enough. Choosing self-preservation over self-sacrifice, he let his weapon fall, then turned and sprinted for the front door. Straining with every muscle, he pumped his arms, aiming towards the broken entrance his team had so recently entered.

Dashing down the hall toward safety, he could still hear the splashing of his final abandoned companion in the pool behind him.

* * *

Outside the baths, twenty men waited. In various degrees of preparation, they milled around the area. Some aimed weapons at the entry, while others moved vehicles into position, pointing their headlights at the front of the building.

The policemen showed no particular concern for the events inside, as each was confident they had sent in the best specialists to do the job. In just a short while, they awaited the capture of the murderer, either bound and alive or as a lump of dead flesh. Calm and self-assured, they appeared relaxed as they carried out preparations to wrap up the night's mission.

The sound of erupting automatic weapon fire from deep inside the building jarred the air of quiet assurance that dominated the area. Worryingly, the chaotic bursts of gunfire continued over the next few moments.

Surprised, the group looked at one another, worry replacing their quiet certainty.

Worse, instead of reports on the situation, only grunts and screams emerged over the squad radio net. More concerned glances were exchanged, and the preparations of the assembled group suddenly became more rushed.

At the back of the group of police, the site commander for the operation was growing nervous. Bald and fierce-looking, the leathery veteran stood near the largest idling vehicle, a command van topped with a collection of antennas.

Red-faced, he called into his radio, "What's going on in there? Report at once."

Only loud scrapes and heavy breaths answered his demand for information. Frustrated, the commander raised his voice and circled a finger in the air, speaking to the assembled cops. "Get ready."

Each waiting officer leveled a weapon at the open door. Pistols, shotguns, and rifles pointed expectantly as worried gazes focused into the darkness beyond the shattered entry.

A terrified voice squawked over the radio, barely audible, "I'm coming out; they're all dead. Don't shoot me."

The cops glanced at each other with alarm. What had recently seemed routine had become decisively abnormal. Fingers poised on triggers, they scanned the doorway.

The retreating officer exited the front, stumbling free from the jagged door. Two policemen ran up and assisted him down the steps, pulling him to safety. The rest of the group waited for the killer, and an uneasy silence settled over the scene.

The site commander leaned closer to his radio, rubbing his smooth scalp in a nervous gesture. Unsure of what to do, he gulped several times. What should have been a moment of triumph over a cop killer had turned into something dreadful and unexpected.

He spoke into his radio with a halting voice, "Command, stiff resistance has been met—"

The spear-wielding Huntsman lunged from the front entryway, moving with unnatural speed for such a large man.

He was met with a hail of gunfire. Rounds pinged off his body, and several direct hits made his head recoil, forcing him backward as he stumbled under the barrage of bullets.

Appearing surprised, the hulking assailant steadied himself, gaining his balance after a few steps.

Recovering, he lifted his bloodied spear and gazed down at the nearest officer. With a start, he hefted his weapon and strode toward a panicked cop, who stumbled backward, even as he blasted away with his pistol.

The sound of the Barrett .50 caliber rifle was deafening, sounding much like a cannon through the night air. Simultaneously, the Huntsman spun from the impact of a massive sniper bullet, falling in a heap on the sidewalk in front of the old baths.

Away from the immediate scene, leaning over the hood of a camouflaged Humvee, a khaki-clad soldier racked back the bolt of the vicious-looking rifle, ejecting a huge spent shell casing from its chamber. The calm soldier worked the bolt forward and eased the enormous stock back into his shoulder. From an elevated parking lot fifty yards away, the soldier really couldn't miss. Crouching behind his formidable weapon, he scanned through its enormous scope, seeking to reacquire the monstrous target.

Jumping to his feet, the Huntsman turned toward the building and fled back inside the bullet-pocked bathhouse. Disappearing from view, he left behind a patch of dark-stained material on the sidewalk where he had fallen.

When he was gone, none of the shocked policemen were eager to follow. Instead, they exchanged confused glances, as if what they just witnessed was some awful waking dream.

Around them, the night grew quiet as the gunfire died away.

Chapter Eight

Laszlo reached into the microwave, an excited look on his expressive face. Wearing large oven mitts, he carefully hauled a bowl of soup out of its tight interior.

Holding his tongue out in concentration, he set the steaming bowl on a plate and, balancing it carefully, carried it to the living room.

Lowering himself into the recliner, he peered at Erica with a beaming smile. With a flushed face, he assumed the look of a guilty boy who had just raided the cookie jar. "You sure you don't want any?"

Erica didn't answer, but her disgusted expression made her feelings about sharing the meal clear. Her revolted gaze drifted over the bubbling concoction, as if she were witnessing the reveal of the world's most vile food tradition.

Snapping his fingers in sudden realization, Laszlo got up and hurried to the kitchen, where he plucked a whole loaf of bread from the cupboard. As he returned to his seat, he grinned at his good fortune.

"You got the good bread from Lipotí Bakery," Laszlo said, his eyes growing eager. "You don't mind if I have a few slices?"

Not responding, Erica cast a look of culinary revulsion. She continued her overwatch of disgust as he dipped a slice of bread into the bubbling jelly-like soup.

"You realize that stuff is like seventy cents at the store?" Erica asked, staring at him with detached fascination as he crammed the gooey sauce-laden bread into his mouth. "And...that literally anything that was actually good for you as an ingredient would be excluded at that price point?"

Laszlo chewed, wrestling with the wonderful taste and holding up a finger to indicate an explanation was forthcoming. Reaching out, he grabbed a glass of soda from the coffee table and washed down the bite with a contented slurp.

"Does it matter?" Laszlo responded, smacking his lips happily. "When something is good, you just got to go with the flow. Don't deny yourself. Don't know how they do it, but this stuff is delicious. Besides, when you kicked me out, I had to learn to cook for myself."

Frowning, Erica pulled her legs under her on the couch. Resting her hands on her knees, she wrinkled her nose.

Shrugging, she realized it was hard to argue with the logic of someone who so thoroughly enjoyed a simple meal like nasty canned soup.

Erica shouldn't have been surprised. She recalled an earlier time when they were first dating, when Laszlo had made an art form out of subsisting on ramen noodles—in all their sodium-soaked glory.

Unlike most college students, who ate such crap in a bid for economic survival, Laszlo had insisted that the noodles were actually delicious and wholly enjoyable.

Consequently, the stroke-inducing dish became a staple of his diet, at least until they moved in together. When she began serving him real food, she had thought his love for the plastic-like noodles had faded away, but now she wasn't so sure.

Erica remembered her happiness at discovering there was no easy way to buy the disgusting noodles over here, as most Hungarians apparently demanded actual nutritional value in their food.

But now, she found herself a bit disappointed that Laszlo had reacquired his love for nutrition-free food.

But now, mulling over that thought, she caught herself and wondered why she cared about what he was now doing.

"Well, you get what you deserve then," Erica said, feigning indifference. "But your early death from eating that garbage is probably going to weigh on my conscience. Not to mention, it might make Monica hate me."

As if on cue, Monica walked in from the hallway. Going to the refrigerator, she rummaged inside and extracted a bag of lunch meat. After fruitlessly looking for something, her confused eyes moved to Laszlo, where she focused on his bag of bread.

Laszlo caught her intent, and he held up two slices of the pricey bread with an angelic smile.

Frowning, Erica cleared her throat, trying for a motherly tone. Instead, she sounded more like a kid picked last for a game at recess. "Mon, I'm sorry if I made you mad. You know I only want what's best—"

"Not talking to you," Monica interrupted, grabbing Laszlo's offered slices. With a moody nod at her dad, she moved back to her room with the impromptu meal.

The door shut, leaving Laszlo sheepishly grinning at Erica.

"You'd think she'd be mad at me," Laszlo said, trying to sound considerate.

Erica chuckled dryly. "She usually is, but I guess missing you is making her anger more broad-based and inclusive. But I suppose that's the least of our worries now."

Nodding, Laszlo became serious, slowly returning to his meal. Glancing up at the muted news on the TV, he looked confused as he chewed and swallowed another hunk of bread. Something seemed to lie on the tip of his thoughts, and he furrowed his brow as he sifted through his memories.

Abruptly, Laszlo pointed to the screen, his eyes going wide. Monica raised her eyebrows in response.

"That's where I've seen that guy. The cop that got killed by the Chain Bridge," Laszlo exclaimed, happy to remember what had bothered him. "He's the guy who pulled Monica and me over the other day and gave me a ticket. Dude was a complete dick."

Erica frowned, moving her disturbed gaze to the TV and back to Laszlo. "That's strange, but that's kind of petty when you consider he just got killed."

Laszlo didn't look convinced, as if something else explained the coincidence. Baffled, he shook his head, trying to understand something.

"Yeah, but it's weird, don't you think?" Laszlo asked.

When Erica didn't respond, Laszlo leaned back in the recliner, eyes pondering. He still held a messy piece of bread in his hand, and as it dangled over the carpet, a splotch of sauce fell onto her white rug below.

Erica bit her tongue, briefly tempted by the suddenly attractive notion of strangling Laszlo.

"I got an idea of what we should do next," Laszlo said, oblivious to his poor manners. "But I have to check with a friend first. We gotta find a way to protect ourselves."

Erica smiled at the notion of him not being there but stifled the urge to send him out on his own. "I'm not sure they'll let you go, Laszlo. Detective Nemeth is a stickler for rules, I think."

Popping the last bit of bread into his mouth, Laszlo responded with a purposeful grin. Somehow, he had suddenly turned into a man of action, or at least a man doing something beyond just sitting on his ass.

Motioning to the world outside the apartment, Laszlo shook his head. "We aren't under arrest. They're welcome to follow me, but I'm not sitting here and waiting to die. And I hope you aren't either."

* * *

Several pots of hot food sat on the stove, simmering in a well-lit kitchen. Steam from each of the cast-iron containers drifted up, clouding a dew-streaked window

156

that ran the length of the area above a chipped countertop.

The kitchen was an old affair, with dated cabinets and orange tiles on the floor resembling ornamentation from the psychedelic sixties. Due to ugly green curtains hanging around the windows, it was as if an interior designer had a stroke while planning the bizarre motif.

Smiling, Viktoria leaned down with a spoon, dipping it into one of the pans. Slowly, she sipped strong paprika gravy, taking her time to allow its aroma to heighten the taste experience.

In her sixties, the plump woman was the archetype of a grandmotherly cook, looking as if she had been plucked whole from a Norman Rockwell painting.

Viktoria smiled at the delicious aroma. Humming softly to herself, she hefted the pan and poured the delectable sauce over a steaming plate of chicken and rice. The gleam in her delighted eyes grew as she inhaled the succulent scent.

Viktoria next leaned down to the oven, peering through the clouded window to check on a browned roll of simmering bread. Satisfied with the plump loaf, she nodded approvingly and turned off the heat.

Everything was going well in her world of perfect home-culinary delights. Such was the case of a committed mother who enjoyed her loving pastime of cooking for a family member.

Contented with the results, Viktoria picked up the plate and moved to the living room door. Nudging it open, she peeked outside of the kitchen into a large, well-lit space.

Adam sat at an extensive computer setup in the middle of the living room. Three large monitors were arranged on a custom desk, powered by a water-cooled computer tower, making him look something like a commanding general in a science fiction movie. On his split screens were scenes of some faraway alien battlefield, with readouts and superimposed maps covering every portion of his first-person game view.

The room itself was modestly furnished with basic furniture and varied rustic paintings, items that were likely used to decorate the apartment long before Adam became a resident.

On the far wall, a windowed set of open doors lead out to a terrace, and bright red curtains were bunched to either side of the balcony. Coupled with a rug that hung down from one of the walls, the room was a cross between Persian decadence and Soviet chic.

Adam was dressed for the part of a reluctant computer warrior, wearing old sweatpants and a loose T-shirt. Two days of stubbly beard growth covered his young features as he concentrated on otherworldly gaming domination.

"Adam, you want some bread to go with your dinner?" Viktoria asked. "You didn't even finish your salad. You have to eat. You need a full, healthy meal."

Adam twisted away from the monitors. The pricey computer chair squeaked, its supports struggling to accommodate his rapid movements and ample frame.

"Mom, I'll have some later. It's kind of hard to diet when you keep cooking new food every five minutes."

Nodding, Viktoria gave a doubtful stare and changed the subject. "Adam, how about that American girl you met? Any luck with that?"

Adam hesitated, then leaned back and laced his fingers behind his head. Turning, he met his mom's gaze and lowered his voice, adopting a reluctant tone. "I liked her a lot, but what you're seeing on the news is happening all around her and her family. The homeless, the cop..."

Adam smiled uneasily—some would have said almost cowardly—as his voice drifted off.

"She's involved with those murders?" Viktoria asked, alarmed.

Adam chuckled and shook his head. "Not involved, but she knows some of the people who have been attacked. So, I'm gonna keep my distance for now."

Surprised, Viktoria thought for a moment. Unsure of what to say, she nodded with a worried frown. "Then stay away from her, honey. Better safe than sorry."

Maintaining a sour expression, Viktoria placed the steaming chicken dinner next to his keyboard. Leaning down, she gave Adam a big smooch, the type reserved for sons of any age.

Moving her robust frame with bountiful energy, she returned to the kitchen to conjure up more calories for his night of gaming.

Adam watched her go. Though he grimaced at being babied, he still appreciated the doting attention, even if he didn't want to show it. Moms worldwide were always moms, wherever and whenever you were.

Smiling to himself, he placed an expensive headset over his ears and rejoined the fight on the screen. Over the next minute, he blasted away at online enemies. Swinging his head left and right, he dodged attacks while also dispatching several virtual foes. His facial expressions were alive and engaged as he battled teenagers and kids across the world in real time.

Suddenly, a surge of wind blew into the room, fluttering his hair and distracting him from the match. Surprised, he frowned and twisted to look at the terrace door. Pausing the game, he tilted his head and scanned the area curiously.

Nothing was there. After a moment, the curtains stopped moving. Puckering his lips, Adam continued to stare toward the balcony, and his gaze locked. Perplexed, his mind searched for something that tugged at his thoughts.

Finally shrugging, he restarted his shooting match by respawning his character. Back in the fight, he dodged with his head as he hunched closer to the computer screens.

A gentle scraping sound came from outside the terrace door, followed by more movement of the old drapes.

His attention now diverted, Adam's eyes locked again on the edge of the room that faced the back of the building. Annoyed, he dropped his headphones and moved toward the terrace. Stopping short of the curtains, he ran his hand over his stubbly chin as he pondered something. Reluctantly, he stepped through the wispy drapes and through the open door.

Outside, the night was brisk and quiet. In the surrounding area, nobody was currently on their balcony, and only the distant sound of jazz emanated from one of the matching terraces. Dull light leaked from the neighbors' porches, making the environment appear lonely from lack of people.

With such a calm area, Adam placed his hands on his hips, breathing in the clean air as he considered the austere surroundings.

Sighing, he shook his head, pushing away the paranoia that had found its way into his normally pragmatic thoughts. Turning, he stepped back inside, where he pivoted to lock the door leading to the balcony. As he engaged the rusted chain into the securing mechanism, he smiled to himself, happy again at the world and his place in it.

Turning back to his computer ensemble, Adam found himself staring into the chest of the much-taller Huntsman. Eyes going wide, he peered up into the unseen face of the enormous man. As he stared, his face froze in terror, his mouth stuck dumbly open.

The Huntsman rammed his razor-sharp knife into Adam's right eye, piercing all the way to the back of his skull with a squishy plunge. With Adam's mouth stuck open, only a faint gurgle accompanied the infliction of the hideous wound.

Adam's head and facial muscles convulsed, and he was raised to his toes as the attacker pressed the blade upward. Blood gushed from his eye, pouring down over his shirt in gouts.

After a few moments, his face stopped twitching, as if Adam had finally settled into a comfortable angle atop the blade. Already dead, his ashen complexion relaxed in death.

With a twist, the Huntsman turned and set the body in the computer chair. Deftly, he sliced off Adam's head with a single cut, making little noise as he pulled the ogling face free of his lower body. With some care, seemingly taking his time to ensure it was done right, the Huntsman placed the detached head in front of the computer monitors and directly next to the still-steaming chicken dinner.

Dipping his gloved fingers into Adam's blood, the Huntsman scrawled the symbol of the Order of Vengeance on the white weathered wall. Quietly opening the balcony door, he quickly exited the room and disappeared over the balcony.

After several quiet moments, Viktoria's blissfully unaware voice called out from the kitchen, "Adam, would you like some jam on your bread?"

Holding a plate of warm bread and beaming with a pleasant smile, Viktoria swung open the door.

* * *

Laszlo kept his head low to avoid being seen as the taxi weaved through the darkness toward the Castle District.

Around the vehicle, crowds of families and tourists from every corner of the world appeared unbothered. Unlike him, they didn't seem worried about the murderous lunatic in the city.

Slowing down, the taxi pulled to an entrance arm that only allowed local cars into the Castle District area. Two policemen stood on either side of it, their expressions unfriendly in the sparse streetlight.

"Sorry, I don't have an entry card anymore," Laszlo said, frowning at a selection of cards in his wallet. "I'll have to walk in from here."

Stepping from the taxi, Laszlo paid the cabbie and glanced around. Nervously, he ducked under the automatic arm and paced up an inclined street toward Erica's distant apartment building.

As he strode ahead, locals were out enjoying the pleasant night air. Gathering along the busy street, families and tourists talked over each other as they took in their active surroundings.

Farther on, Laszlo squeezed through crowds of nearby residents, many of whom he recognized. But not all of those with familiar faces returned his kind smile. In response, he frowned at being ignored by some people who knew him, which was undoubtedly due to the reasons behind his divorce from Erica.

Looking forlorn, Laszlo wondered why some people had such a hard time forgiving others. These former neighbors had undoubtedly blamed him for the breakup in his relationship with Erica.

In reality, the divorce had truly been his fault, but he was also sorry for everything. He had even gone out of his way to try to make amends, going so far to individually seek his neighbors out to express his apologies.

But no luck, because they still had given him the cold shoulder. Finally, Laszlo just had to give up, accepting the fact that those "friends" were all lost to him now. It really sucked, even if it really wasn't any of their business. *I'm a good guy. Why can't they just get over it?*

As Laszlo approached his former apartment, he saw that something was terribly wrong. The cops at the entrance to the building had intense, sad expressions, as if mourning lost family members. One young officer even had the puffy-eyed appearance of someone who had been crying. *What happened?*

Laszlo waved politely as he walked by the protective detail, but once inside, he hurried his pace and avoided the elevator. Angling to the side, he ascended a set of stairs in the lobby. His eyes grew panicked as he bounded up the steps, worrying more with each passing second.

Bursting through the staircase on Erica's floor, Laszlo almost broke into a run toward her door. Growing more alarmed with each stride, he willed everything to be okay as he approached the apartment.

As he got close, the door was thrown open, and Erica stared out at him. Dumbfounded and sad, she peered with watery eyes and a long despondent face. Breathing carefully, she raised her hand and wiped away snot with a wad of crumpled tissues.

Hurrying up, Laszlo had to stop himself from reaching out to comfort her. Barely able to speak, his voice came out in a low whisper. "What's wrong?"

Erica turned around, looking back into the apartment without answering. Stepping numbly inside, Laszlo followed her in. To the left, his gaze fell on Monica.

His daughter sat on the couch, confused and sad. She looked more like a scared young girl than before, with a vacant, fearful expression and forlorn eyes.

Catching himself, Laszlo was troubled by Monica's frightened new expression. For a girl that knew mostly sarcasm and realism, she showed an understanding of life that was far beyond her age. But now she looked like a sheltered and very sad child.

Overwhelmed, Monica nodded a frightened hello, but for the moment she avoided talking. Her young mind, grasping at the horrors surrounding them and their adopted city, had withdrawn from the present. Much like a glass that can only take so much water, her face showed a persona filled to capacity with too much stress and worry.

On the other side of the room, Erica walked to peer out the window. Trying to shield her distraught, tear-streaked face from view, she crossed her arms and stood quietly. Staring blankly, she ignored the busy square below.

Sitting at the kitchen table, Nemeth sat with a coffee cup. He watched Laszlo with his eternally observant gaze, the kind that made a person feel like all their secrets were laid bare. Fortunately, Laszlo had no secrets to hide; his sins and weaknesses were known by all.

Nemeth clinked his coffee cup with a stirring spoon, adding sugar in controlled amounts with a gentle circling motion. Each movement had an annoyingly precise quality.

"What happened?" asked Laszlo, exasperated. "Is everyone okay?"

Continuing to face away from him, Erica's chin quivered. She merely shook her head without speaking.

"Unfortunately, no," replied Nemeth, his voice emotionless. "Mrs. Varga's friend, Adam, has been found in his apartment. Dead. His mother, Viktoria Molnar, has been hospitalized."

Erica turned around and moved to Monica. Reaching down, she absently stroked her daughter's hair. Her expression lost in grief and guilt, she maintained her detached bearing.

"Mr. Molnar was staged, like the other victims," Nemeth continued, "and his mother has been traumatized so severely that she will need medical care...for an extended time."

Astonished, Laszlo glanced back and forth between Erica and Monica, unsure of whom to comfort more—or even if either of them would want him to.

"How can that be?" asked Laszlo, struggling with the dark news. "I thought you had him cornered last night?"

"We thought we did as well, Mr. Varga," answered Nemeth, his chin set in a determined frown. "But he got away. The Gellért Baths have ancient sewers that run underneath them. We're assuming that is how he fled."

Nemeth motioned vaguely out the window, a hint of frustration in his voice. "We just don't have any answers. We now have a total of four dead police officers, yet we still can't determine who did it—or why."

Shocked, Laszlo kept his stupefied gaze on Nemeth, trying to absorb the information. "Four? How is this guy doing this? Don't you have like every gun on Earth? Is he a ghost?"

Suddenly, Erica turned from her daughter and walked to Laszlo. Leaning into him, she hugged her surprised ex, embracing him with awkward sadness. Apparently, she needed to be comforted, and for now, Laszlo would have to do.

Surprised, Laszlo returned the embrace, glad for the attention, even if the cause was not out of joy for his presence.

After a quiet moment, Monica returned to her senses and focused on her parents. Confused, her face lost the sadness of minutes before and gained a hint of annoyance.

Erica became self-conscious of her daughter's attention. Disengaging curtly from Laszlo, she faced Nemeth. "Is he a ghost, this killer?" she asked, her face flushed. "Or...something else?"

Nemeth wasn't surprised by the question. In fact, he looked as if he had been thinking the same thing. "I'm not sure what I believe right now. The suspect, by our count, has been shot at least a hundred times, with some of the most powerful weapons available."

Erica and Laszlo exchanged alarmed glances. Neither was knowledgeable about guns, but survival under such damage didn't seem likely.

Nemeth continued in a grave voice. "And he still hasn't stopped his murderous activities. The only thing we can tell is that he has some kind of extreme armor."

"Armor?" Erica asked, perplexed. "What kind of armor can withstand that kind of punishment? I'm no expert, but I've never heard of anything that stops bullets like that."

Sighing, Nemeth shook his head, equally confused. "We don't know. Bits of some hard material have been found where he was shot, along with some kind of black fluid that doesn't appear to be blood. We're having it tested, but it will take time."

Rubbing his jaw, Nemeth pointed to Erica and addressed Laszlo in the same monotone voice. "Mrs. Varga has told us about a group of fanatics from four hundred years ago, this so-called 'Order of

Vengeance.' Perhaps there is now a modern version of these maniacs running around, dressing up and killing people. We think they could be behind this. If we can find them soon, we can end this madness."

Confused, Laszlo glanced at Erica. She shook her head at his unspoken question. "I'll tell you later, Laszlo. It's a long story."

Stretching, Nemeth moved close to the former couple, keeping his tone low so Monica couldn't easily hear. "This would explain how some lunatics were murdering people. But unfortunately, it doesn't explain how or why they're choosing their victims."

Gesturing to the entire apartment, Nemeth continued with a voice that made it clear he was open to suggestions. "Many of the victims are connected to this place. To this *family*."

Erica placed her hands on her hips, shaking her head. "Yes, but why? Why...kill Adam and the Horvaths? Why attack Laszlo? It doesn't make any sense."

"I wish I knew, for all of our sakes," Nemeth answered, his features dour. "But I learned this a long time ago: In this job, violent and crazy people sometimes don't need a reason. At least, not a reason that normal people can understand. It's the nature of their madness."

Monica stood and approached the group of adults. She leaned close to her parents, not understanding what was going on. "Are we going to be killed too, Mom?"

There was silence for a while as the four people, young and old, looked sympathetically at one another. None of the adults apparently had an answer, at least not an honest one.

Breathing deeply, Erica shook her head and focused on her daughter with an uncertain, humorless grin. "No, we're certainly not. We'll find a way to get through this."

Thinking intently, Erica took some time to ponder her family's future, her face moving through shades of doubt, worry, and finally, resoluteness.

Suddenly feeling assertive, she looked over at Nemeth. With her eyes locked on his, her voice grew bolder. "We're going to get out of this city, Detective, until this psycho is caught. Laszlo has family in Eger."

She turned her questioning eyes to Laszlo. "Family that we can stay with?"

Nemeth considered Erica's words, running through options in his head. Slowly, he offered a reluctant smile. "I understand your feelings. I also understand the worries you must feel, Mr. and Mrs. Varga. This is a lot to go through for a family. But you also must consider this whole situation is bigger than you. In many ways, it is affecting the entire city. Two million people need this murderer caught or killed."

Erica frowned, doubtful. "What does that mean, Detective?"

"It means," Nemeth replied, hesitating, "that I'm sending men with you, wherever you're going—unless you prefer to be taken into protective custody."

Frustrated, Erica glanced toward her daughter and Laszlo, awaiting their reactions. With no response, she sighed deeply.

Turning back to Nemeth, she lowered her voice and spoke soberly. "Detective, no offense intended, but your men can't seem to defend themselves, much less protect our small family."

Raising her tone, Erica tried to project some optimism. "Besides, our best protection will be going somewhere nobody knows us, where nobody can find us. If you send people with us, this nut might be able to follow. As of now, only you know what city we'll be near."

Picking up his cup from the table, Nemeth considered her words as he sipped the last of his coffee. Nodding, he shrugged and allowed himself a grim smile. "When will you leave?"

Erica looked between Laszlo and Monica, studying each of their features as she considered their chances and the need to move quickly.

Nemeth slowly watched the disjointed family, his doubtful gaze indicating what he thought of their plan. With no immediate response, he retrieved his coat, shrugging it on as he awaited their reply.

"Tomorrow morning," Erica finally said, staring directly at Laszlo, and for once in a long time, showing no animosity toward her former cheating spouse. "If that's okay with you?"

With worried expressions, first Laszlo and then Monica both nodded, silently agreeing to Erica's proposed departure.

Chapter Nine

The midday sun peeked from behind the overcast sky, throwing shadows over the dumpy eastern suburbs of Budapest. Exhaust fumes from meandering traffic and a pall of overhead smog added an extra smattering of potent haze to the gray afternoon backdrop.

Glancing down at the map on her mobile phone, Erica squinted as she compared it with the surrounding streets. Frustrated, she raised her gaze to linger on the depressing apartment blocks to either side of their slow-moving line of traffic.

Erica peered over and huffed at Laszlo, who drove with a sullen look pasted on his irritated features.

"I've never been this far east," said Erica. "Everything looks the same with these crappy old buildings."

Laszlo frowned, pointing up to the right. He was no more enamored with the area than Erica and gave a disappointed nod at a group of dejected pedestrians on a nearby sidewalk. It was as if communal depression was necessary for residency in this area.

"Half of the GPS coordinates are wrong; they changed the building numbers, and Google still has them wrong," replied Laszlo. "I think number forty-seven is coming in another street or two. This reminds me why I never wanted to live in Zuglo."

The street ahead was potholed, and grass in the open fields around them was unkempt and interspersed with weeds and discarded plastic bags. The rubbish and overgrown vegetation in the vacant lots seemed appropriate in front of doddering concrete-paneled apartment structures.

On the motorway, cars and delivery vans were stopped, their drivers unconcerned about blocking traffic. Farther ahead, road construction had blocked off one lane, but no actual repair was underway on the cracked and broken asphalt. Instead, the construction cones and warning signs left by the highway department appeared to be abandoned.

"There," shouted Erica, gesturing at a distant walk-up restaurant next to a rundown parking lot. "I should've known you would choose such a fine restaurant to meet someone."

Feeling offended, Laszlo frowned at Erica. She responded with a playful grin, offering an unusual look of good humor.

Pulling through another intersection, Laszlo stayed in the right lane and turned into a gravel parking area next to the food joint. Engaging the emergency break, he left the engine running as they waited.

The broken-down restaurant had signs advertising *Pizza* and *Kebab*, but Erica would have been surprised if a side of *Hepatitis A* wasn't also included.

"Mom, can we get something to eat?" asked Monica, raising her voice from the back seat. "Dad made breakfast, and the eggs tasted funny."

"Not even if that was the last food on Earth," answered Erica, her lip curling at the idea of consuming such street fare. She had never been one to embrace food snobbery, but when it came to her daughter's health, she could never be too careful.

Laszlo chuckled, shaking his head and smiling. "Don't know what you're missing. Finer cuisine has never been made."

"Where did you meet Zoltan?" asked Erica, changing the subject to avoid feeling ill. "I've never seen him before, at least that I can remember. Not that I care…but obviously he's not here yet…so give me the story."

"He was my sponsor at my AA meetings," said Laszlo, peering meekly over at Erica. "He owns a bar in the seventh district, which is kind of weird, but once you know him, it kind of makes sense. He figures testing your demons keeps your resistance at its best."

"An alcoholic who owns a bar and serves drinks to drunks? Sounds lovely," said Erica, clearly unimpressed.

"I said it was weird, but it makes sense," Laszlo said, sounding like a preacher spreading the good word. "You ever notice that people with the best immune systems are those who strengthen them by living in grime and squalor? It's the same idea, at least when you hear him explain it."

"That doesn't really sound scientific, Laszlo. In fact, it sounds like one of the dumbest things I've ever heard."

Laszlo shrugged, as if it were her own loss for refusing to accept the self-evident wisdom. "Every time I'm about to slide back, he's there for me. Just recently, he said he'd kill me if I gave up and started drinking again. He's one of those guys who'll do anything for you."

Erica nodded, speaking in an ironic voice. "I'm sure he would, but he'd have been a better friend if he taught you how to avoid bimbos—instead of just booze."

Laszlo glanced back at Monica and pleaded with his eyes at Erica: *Please don't, I beg you.*

Erica shrugged, enjoying the torture. "You did what you did, Laszlo. Don't act like a saint now."

Finally interrupting her torment of Laszlo, Erica became distracted, noticing a homeless guy begging near the sidewalk restaurant. The shoddily dressed man, covered in ill-fitting rags and sporting a thick gray beard, didn't seem interested in the food a customer offered him. Apparently, he preferred cold hard cash.

Erica couldn't blame the homeless dude. Silently, she reminded herself to never again give garbage food to beggars. Nobody, even the starving homeless, deserved the unique misery and slow death of eating that god-awful street food.

Monica stuck her head up between the front seats. Looking cheery, she rotated her gaze between her parents. After some consideration, she let her stare wander back to her father. "What's a bimbo?"

Confounded, Laszlo stumbled through his words, his face a mix of guilt and parental agony. "Well, it's a word that... um..."

"It was a bad woman that Daddy was friends with," said Erica, finally coming to Laszlo's rescue.

Despairing for a moment, Laszlo's face brightened as he tried to drum up his best counterpoint. He even managed to put on his best insurance-salesman smile. "But not anymore. Daddy's a better man now."

Erica wrinkled her nose, looking doubtful as she tousled Monica's hair. Her approval of Laszlo's current behavior and excuses was hardly more positive than two years ago, when he had so thoroughly destroyed any notion of happiness in her world. "Uh-huh, Laszlo...sure you are."

Monica continued her confused look, gazing between Laszlo and Erica with curious eyes.

"There's Zoltan," shouted Laszlo, relief flooding his face as he pointed to the parking lot's entrance.

Laszlo hopped out of the car and moved toward a white panel van pulling into the parking lot. Swinging in a belated circle, the van backed toward his car, pulling within a few feet of Laszlo's trunk as a haze of polluting smoke erupted from its tailpipe.

Getting out, Erica and Monica gathered together, watching the dented van with interest. Frowning, they awaited whatever might emerge from the dented vehicle.

Zoltan, enormous and tall, stepped from the front seat, clambering out the driver's side with surprising agility. Despite his immense size, each step and movement was fluid, and his bearing gave the impression of calculated motion, like every effort he made was carefully considered.

Offering a huge grin and a steady handshake to Laszlo, his bushy beard didn't quite hide his radiant smile and crooked teeth.

Clapping Laszlo's shoulder, he moved on and approached Erica with a respectful nod. "Laszlo, is this your family?"

Laszlo smiled and nodded intensely, his face a mix of pride and sadness. Staying quiet, he watched the unfolding meeting with a depressed smile.

Zoltan held out his bear paw of a hand to mother and daughter, shaking both gently. Erica was surprised by his size and friendliness, while Monica simply stared up at the imposing man in wonder.

Zoltan leaned toward Laszlo, winking at Erica and speaking loud enough for everyone to hear. "Well, aren't you the biggest idiot who ever lived? Your ex is beautiful—and kind."

Laszlo frowned at Zoltan, his smile wilting. "Thanks...buddy."

"No problem. I'm always here to help, you know that," said Zoltan, now winking at Monica, who hid precariously behind Erica.

Rubbing his hands together, Zoltan motioned to the back of his dingy van, his grin growing wider. It was the type of grin that could make you happy, even if you had just witnessed an execution.

Zoltan's infectious enthusiasm forced an unwanted smile onto Erica's lips. She suddenly felt her mood brightening.

"Now, look what I have for you," said Zoltan, yanking open the rusty, bent door with a mild screech.

Inside, the afternoon light illuminated a dirty blanket on the floor of the dark interior. The Varga family traded worried glances, as if daring one another to be the first to peek beneath it.

Keeping his expectant smile, Zoltan moved the blanket aside, revealing a monstrous rifle. It had two barrels and was carved with various animals on its silver-clad metal exterior. Without a doubt, even to untrained eyes, it was a serious weapon for serious times.

Erica's grin faded as she processed the strange scene. A huge man presenting a huge rifle wasn't to be expected every day, even in the bizarre series of events that had become her normal life.

"This is a .470 Nitro Express, one of the most powerful rifles in the world," Zoltan said, and something like unrestrained joy emanated from his features. "It can shoot a five-hundred-grain bullet more than two thousand feet per second."

Zoltan leaned into the van, picking up the weapon to admire its impressive dimensions and awesome potential. As he caressed the fine-wooden stock, Laszlo fixated on its elegant design, joining Zoltan in his admiration.

Behind them, Erica frowned at the mesmerized men and their deadly toy.

"Oh, and those are the bullets you wanted," Zoltan added, pointing at a cardboard box as he returned the rifle to the blanket. "Solid, hard ammo. These won't deform when they hit bone."

Standing back, Zoltan flashed a brilliant smile, looking like a grinning sasquatch. His pleasant mood was buoyant and enthusiastic as he continued. "There's nothing in the world this gun won't kill. It's a real beast. It's not politically correct to say nowadays, but that gun has actually dropped a charging rhino."

Confused, Erica frowned. "I can't imagine we'll need to shoot such a thing here—in Hungary."

"Maybe not," Zoltan responded, his jovial features turning cagey. "But sometimes there are worse monsters in the world than the wild ones."

Nodding, Laszlo wrapped the blanket around the rifle and ammunition, cradling it carefully as he carried it to his car.

After stuffing everything gently in the trunk, Laszlo returned to face Zoltan. His eyes were misty as he looked up at the big man.

"Thanks, Zoltan. You're a real pal," Laszlo said, hugging him like an appreciative child. "I don't know what I'd do without you."

Laszlo held the embrace with his hulking friend longer than most men would. Zoltan didn't appear to mind, and he patted Laszlo on the back several times before they finally pulled apart.

"Any time, I'm always here for you," Zoltan said sincerely. "Happy hunting."

With that, Zoltan moved toward Erica and her daughter. He hugged Erica briefly, whispering so Monica and Laszlo couldn't hear. "Be strong and take care of him. He's been a real asshole, but he means well. We all need help in life—and someone to give us a second chance."

Unsure of how to respond, Erica stayed silent, weighing Zoltan's words for sincerity and how they applied to her and Laszlo's particular situation. Gently nodding, she decided in favor of Zoltan's good intentions and relaxed her expression into a kind smile.

Zoltan stepped back, holding Erica at arm's length and appraising her with an honest grin. Finishing the interaction, he reached over and pinched Monica's cheek, eliciting a grin from the suddenly happy girl.

With a final wave to Laszlo, he turned and hopped into his weathered vehicle. When the van coughed to life, he quickly steered it back onto the broken street, wading back into traffic and toward the middle of Budapest.

Erica watched him go with a bemused tilt of her head. Feeling like she just witnessed the passing of an unknown force, she couldn't help but feel affected by Zoltan's strange charisma.

Turning back to Laszlo, Erica somehow felt better for the encounter. "Well, that was interesting. For the first time ever, I liked a friend of yours."

* * *

Continuous fields of wheat stretched to either side of the freeway, making the extended horizon feel uninhabited and eternal. Above, the sky was partially blue, with fast-moving clouds shading the sun at regular intervals.

It was a nice day, but Erica was getting a bit of a *Children-of-the-Corn* vibe from the empty fields around their motoring car.

Frowning, Laszlo pressed his Saab along the divided highway, passing a large combine harvester that was partially on the interstate. Erica sat in the passenger seat with her feet kicked up, staring out over the endless rows of grain while she mentally reviewed the long-ago horror film.

Laszlo, stuck in a dour mood, was openly irritated by her feet-on-the-dashboard breach of etiquette and glared over. The lack of manners was made worse due to the fact they both knew she was doing it on purpose.

Dragging his eyes back to the road, he calmed himself, controlling his annoyance at her efforts to sully his precious car. He was generally a man who held no pretentions with anyone, especially Erica, but his car was really his only possession on Earth he considered sacrosanct.

Relenting, Erica moved her feet down and peered curiously into the distance. Farther past the staple of grain crops were green hills and distant mountains, spaced out and towering on the periphery of the Great Hungarian Plain.

"So let me get this straight," Erica said, scowling as she pondered earlier events. "He just happens to have a rhino gun lying around his house? How does that work?"

Laszlo kept his eyes on the road, chuckling as he considered their encounter with Zoltan. Glancing in the rearview mirror, he noted Monica taking a nap in the back seat before answering. "He is one of those people with an interesting life, and by interesting, I mean I don't know how much of what he does would be considered strictly legal. I really don't ask."

"That must make for absorbing stories when you hang out," Erica replied, and for once, she looked intrigued to hear such stories. "It gets boring working in academia, where so much of the world is controlled and sterile. Real living can be a different experience."

With a guarded smile, Laszlo nodded. "Okay, the story is, he was in the French Foreign Legion. That's interesting by itself when you think about it, but the rumor is he got kicked out because, during a battle somewhere or other, it seemed he liked fighting a little too much. They couldn't control him."

Arching an eyebrow, Erica offered a skeptical frown. "I thought people went into that unit to escape their past, to start a new life. I heard they even accepted Nazis after World War Two. Never heard of someone leaving the Legion to escape anything. That sounds backwards."

Laszlo tilted his head. "I don't know about that. But I know not many Nazis would have messed with

Zoltan—unless they were suicidal. It may all be BS, but I've heard him speaking French, and he does seem to know a lot about weapons."

Erica leaned back, lost in thought. "Whatever his story, I can see he has notions of redeeming himself, which is probably why he works so hard to help you. It's likely why he wants to save you from yourself, I suppose."

Laszlo didn't respond, merely flashing a defensive glance her way. He clearly didn't like where the conversation was going.

"There's a problem with those ideas of redemption, unfortunately," Erica continued, trying to hide her bitterness. "It focuses on the person who destroyed the lives of others, making them into a victim. It does nothing for those who had to live with the effects of the evil crap done to them earlier. Those other people get to live with the results, and nobody talks about their destroyed lives. Instead, everyone rushes to forgive the bastard who caused the problem."

Laszlo blanched, recoiling from her unhidden potshots. Staying quiet, he avoided her gaze, not wanting another serving of verbal ass-whooping. The mirth disappeared from his eyes as he stared quietly ahead, watching the blurry images of the remote freeway roll past.

Going silent, Erica peered back out her window to the countryside. Not having more to say, she resumed her far-off stare at the rural, flat landscape.

* * *

As the car wound down the long dirt road, a plume of dust billowed behind them. Pressing into the late-afternoon shadows, Laszlo drove incautiously. Rocks sprayed up from his wheels as he embraced his inner disregard for speed limits.

Above, the sky had darkened, and tumultuous dark-gray clouds swirled above the rural backdrop. Due to the stretch of dark sky, the environment had taken on a menacing look.

Despite the foreboding weather, Erica looked up at a hill running parallel with the road. Up the sloping side ran rows of grapevines. Nodding at the quaint and productive landscape, she realized that it would have been a lovely place to bring Monica in the recent past.

"Pretty nice area, Laszlo," Erica said, moving her gaze from the sloping vineyards to a flat upcoming area of cherry trees. "Yet another thing you never bothered to show me."

Laszlo grinned, trying to make light of a visit to his uncle, one that never happened while they were married. For some reason, he didn't see that as his fault.

"You missed out on a lot more than this," Laszlo exclaimed. "My family has owned property all around Eger for hundreds of years, just family after family making a humble living here."

Erica nodded as her eyes swept the scenery, focusing on flowers and trees with a detached, almost mournful smile. "I missed more than that, undoubtedly. But you're right, life does seem to flash by."

"What's that mean?" asked Laszlo.

"Well, look at it like this," Erica explained, gesturing to the menagerie of scrubby vegetation and groves around them. "If you had lived here four hundred years ago, you would have grown up, married, and been buried in some long-forgotten grave by now. You probably would've worked these fields until your hands bled."

Erica paused, trying to envisage what life must have been like back then. All those old distant faces and lives, lost to time. Each of those nameless people had their own ambitions and pursuits. It was a depressing thought, but it was also noble in a working-person sort of way.

"Anyway, everyone in that period, lord and peasant alike, is gone and forgotten, unless they ended up in some obscure history book in one of the university's boring libraries."

"Okay, so people live and die. Nothing crazy about that," replied Laszlo, not bothering to think too deeply about her words.

Nodding, Erica continued.

"Yeah, but every one of those people, from the most humble to the most exalted, had an interesting story. They cherished life and were looking for happiness. Unlike us, they probably found it, too, because they didn't have Hollywood and the internet selling them ridiculous expectations about what it means to live a happy life. I'm sure their definition of success would have been much different than today."

Frowning, Laszlo raised an eyebrow. "That's pretty deep, but it doesn't tell me what you're getting at."

Erica lowered her voice, showing a frustrated frown.

"My point is this: We're here for only a while, Laszlo, and not one of us is more important than some peasant from centuries ago. The only thing that matters is how you make your life and how well you treat those around you. Technology, traveling to see the Taj Mahal, partying at some tropical resort, becoming a billionaire—none of those things matter."

Laszlo locked his jaw at her words, trying to process her meaning as he mulled over their current situation. Staying quiet, for once he was at a loss for words.

"How well you treat those around you," Erica repeated, staring down the long road as a remote farmhouse came into view.

Erica pointed to the upcoming house. It was a sprawling two-story home with colorfully tiled roofs and miles of surrounding grass and trees. A couple in their sixties stood in front of the house's wooden fence, smiling at the incoming car.

Monica, silent until now, leaned forward and also pointed. Erica and Laszlo were both surprised, having thought she was fast asleep.

"That's Uncle Jozsef," Monica shouted, her voice a mixture of fascination and excitement. "What a cool place."

After they pulled up, Monica scrambled out of the car. Smiling, her bright eyes scanned the orchards and surrounding foliage, ecstatic at the potential to explore.

Emerging with less enthusiastic demeanors, Erica and Laszlo walked up to the older couple.

Jozsef was weathered and stooped, but he also had a gleam of excitement under his array of wrinkles. His wife Dori was of similar age and bearing, but her skin was less affected by decades of sunlight. Standing together, they looked as if they were posing for a rural postcard.

Jozsef stepped forward, and his big grin made his wrinkles even more pronounced.

"Laszlo, it's been a long time," Jozsef said, spreading his arms to indicate the whole wide property. "Welcome to my home."

Laszlo eagerly moved forward to embrace the couple, showing his happiness and appreciation for the visit. They mingled in greeting for several long moments, exchanging hugs.

Moving on from Laszlo, Jozsef bent down to smile at Monica's face. With a gentle effort, he pinched her cheek with a calloused hand.

"And how is your pretty daughter?" asked Jozsef, moving his grin from Monica up to Erica. "She looks more like her beautiful mom every day."

Monica frowned with an *eww, old people* look, while Erica blushed at the compliment.

Looking shy, Erica stepped closer to their hosts.

Dori met Erica's gaze, speaking in a kind tone as she flashed a yellow-toothed smile. "Glad to have you here, Erica. Nice to meet you at last. Sorry that it took...so long."

Keeping her polite look, Erica offered a genuine grin to Dori, then Jozsef.

"Thank you for having us on such short notice," said Erica, peering around the exterior of the home with an impressed face. "It's a beautiful home and property."

Nodding at the compliment, Jozsef moved to the back of the car. Opening the trunk, he began unloading bags to carry inside. Laying their luggage on the ground, he stacked the well-packed belongings in good order.

"Let's get you all inside, and we can catch up on everything," said Jozsef, his mood growing enthusiastic at hosting family.

Dori, Monica, and Erica walked inside through a metal gate in the fence, while Jozsef continued to unload the back of the vehicle. Laszlo stepped close to help, but when Jozsef saw his enormous rifle under the blanket, he looked up with a concerned expression.

Laszlo smiled reluctantly, gesturing to the large firearm with an apologetic shrug. Speaking slowly, he switched to Hungarian. "There's a lot to tell, so I hope you won't be too bothered by it. It's got to be the craziest thing you've heard—or ever will hear."

* * *

The police headquarters was less busy than before. Most of the tables and desks in the big hall were empty, and only a skeleton crew of public safety personnel remained.

The entire area was still brightly lit, as if it were a sports stadium awaiting fans. Some officers clacked away at computer terminals, while others talked on the phone or filled out paperwork. Only the mild hiss of a wall-mounted air conditioner accompanied the occasional murmur of fatigued voices.

Nemeth stood near his situation board, focusing intently as he peered up. He held up a scribbled note and stared at the writing, comparing it with doodles and pins on the larger map above.

On Nemeth's desk near the corner, several open police folders were stacked. Nearby, large crime scene photos were scattered over the rest of the available desk space. Moving his gaze to the photos of blood splotches and torn flesh, he breathed deeply and rubbed his eyes.

"You need to get some rest, Detective," Kovacs said, rising from his nearby desk. "You haven't slept in two days. You might not like it, but being tired makes you worse at your job, not better."

Nemeth frowned at the suggestion, but he couldn't disagree. With his dark-circled, bloodshot eyes, he resembled an exhausted ghoul.

"You may be right, but our killer won't sympathize with my sleep habits," Nemeth replied. Turning to the map, he pointedly changed the subject. "Sergeant, what makes this crazy bastard so hard to catch?"

Kovacs thought for a moment, shaking his head as he gestured toward the map. Acting like it was a trick question, he played along with his boss' thought experiment. "Well, he just seems to appear everywhere, like he's transported straight out of *Star Trek*. There's no trace of him outside the crime scenes."

Nemeth crossed his arms, nodding slightly in agreement. "And nobody notices him, wherever he goes. Even though he looks like a freak and dresses like he works in a carnival."

Kovacs walked up to the map. Pointing at a red pin for each of the murder sites, he clicked his tongue and sighed.

Reaching on top of a nearby cabinet, Kovacs grabbed a red marker. Carefully, he drew a line between each of the spots where the violent crimes occurred. Using the tip of his finger, he softly counted the distances between them. "You're right, of course. It doesn't make sense. Where does he live? He must know people, take the subway, and move about somehow."

Chewing his lip, Nemeth concentrated on the map. Reaching out, he snatched the marker from Kovac's hand and circled each of the pins with a thick red line. Staring at the center of the updated map, his eyes sharpened.

Glancing from the side, Kovacs made eye contact, his unspoken query focusing directly on Nemeth: *What are we going to do, Lieutenant?*

"The answer has to be in the Castle District," Nemeth said. His voice suddenly determined, his mood brightened, like he was on the verge of assembling a final piece to some vague puzzle.

Tossing the pen back to Kovacs, he grew upbeat. "I missed something there. The Vargas live there, and somehow, it's centered on them. We just have to find the connection."

Kovacs was skeptical. "And just wandering over there will somehow lead us to the killer?"

Nemeth chuckled softly, looking philosophical for the moment. "The salary isn't great, but solving crimes is what they pay us for, wherever we have to go. Whatever we have to do."

Grunting, Nemeth leaned over and collected his coat from the chair. Slipping on the ruffled overcoat, he faced Kovacs with a determined frown. "I'm going to get some sleep and head back to the Castle District in the morning. Meet me there at nine a.m....and call me if anything happens in the meantime. I've had enough of being a half-step behind this psychopath."

Kovacs nodded glumly as Nemeth paced out of the headquarters. Peering back at the map, his eyes focused on the red circle surrounding tomorrow's meeting location.

Chapter Ten

A polished wooden table stood in the middle of the living room, surrounded by solid, well-crafted chairs. Throughout the rest of the area were attractive cabinets and wall decorations, each rustic enough to make the environment feel livable and homey.

Somewhat out of place, a stuffed boar with menacing tusks posed from the corner, its head arched as if ready to roar at any interlopers in the room. Curiously, its glassy eyes appeared less intimidating, and it glared inquisitively from its metal mounting base, almost as if the beast was unhappy about its odd placement in death.

Gentle lamps illuminated the entire space, casting a warm reflective sheen on the furniture.

The Varga family sat around the roomy table, their expectant eyes fixed on a large pot. Steam rose from the massive container, and the comfort-food image was heightened by Jozsef's smile as he stirred its contents with a large ladle.

"Ahh, goulash," said Jozsef, peering down with the eyes of a soup connoisseur. "Hungary's perfect gift to the world."

Still smiling at the food, Jozsef ladled servings from the pot into pottery bowls and passed them gently around the table. As each helping of the meaty stew was placed before the family, they licked their lips in growing anticipation.

To add to the intensive culinary experience, Dori slid several plates of freshly baked bread next to each bowl.

"Eat all you want," Dori said, her smile widening. "We have plenty more, and dessert is in the oven: layered cake for our hungry guests."

Erica deeply inhaled the exquisite scent of the bubbling stew. The heavenly aroma forced her mind and cravings into a kind of food-loving nirvana, where her feelings of impending bliss could only be satisfied by rampant gorging. Normally circumspect when it came to food, she hadn't realized how hungry she had been.

Thinking more on the subject, it always struck Erica that people who cooked great food were often the happiest folks in the world, as if their love of life somehow heightened the flavor of their cooking.

"This is honestly like eating perfection," Erica said, moving her appreciative gaze between Dori and Jozsef. "You didn't have to go to all this effort for our sakes."

Dori answered with a contented nod, clearly happy that they enjoyed her cooking. She expectantly moved her gaze to Monica, who had just taken a spoonful of the stew. As Monica's eyes glazed over in delight, Dori's grin widened further.

Walking over to a large cabinet, Jozsef withdrew a simple bottle of clear liquid from a drawer. Holding it up with a large grin, he returned to the table. To his side, Dori pushed several clinking shot glasses next to her husband.

"Not just goulash. We have pálinka, homemade and with just the right amount of aging," Jozsef said, his demeanor delighted. "This one is five years old. I've been saving it for just the right occasion."

Lining up the glasses in front of Erica and Laszlo, Jozsef first poured a generous shot for Erica. When he moved to Laszlo, he was surprised to see his nephew cover the glass with his hand.

Politely, Laszlo shook his head and pointed to a pitcher of apple cider on one of the nearby cabinets. "I'll just have juice, if that's okay."

Surprised, Jozsef nodded, then poured two shots for Dori and himself. He made brief eye contact with Dori as he passed her a glass, unspoken concern passing between them.

"Now, tell me about this nasty business in Budapest," said Jozsef. "What made you hurry way out here to us?"

Laszlo met Jozsef's gaze, considering what to tell his uncle. Quickly deciding, he kept his voice low and clear. "Most of it, you've probably seen on TV. There's a maniac on the loose, and the police can't seem to catch him. Or better yet, kill the sick bastard."

Surprised, Dori stared directly at Laszlo, then looked over at Monica, unsure if it was appropriate to speak in front of the young girl. Both Laszlo and Erica nodded, silently approving an open discussion.

"We saw everything on the news," Dori finally said, taking the initiative to speak before Jozsef. "But why are you running away from the city? There are two million people there. And...plenty of police to protect you?"

Laszlo smiled, flashing a playful grin at Jozsef before continuing. "You were always the smart one. For some reason, this lunatic is targeting us specifically."

Even more confused, Dori tilted her head. "Why you? Who did you make angry?"

Belatedly, Erica interjected, gesturing specifically to Monica, Laszlo, and then herself. "We have no idea. But this nutcase is attacking a lot of people we know and...killing them."

Erica peered down at her stew, suddenly losing her raging appetite from moments before. Unfortunately, a psychopathic murderer and the memories it brought back didn't make for an enjoyable family feast.

Across the table, Dori and Jozsef exchanged concerned glances.

Laszlo addressed their concerns, raising his voice slightly, gesturing toward his daughter and ex-wife. "Nobody knows we're here—not even most of the police. We just need to hide for a while, until they catch this crazy fu--, I mean...person."

Deep in thought, Jozsef gazed at his nephew. Downing a shot, he paused, processing the bizarre news. Reaching over, he slowly poured a second glass of pálinka, taking his time to fill it to the rim of the smokey glass. "You are always welcome here, you know that. You and your family. Always."

Erica frowned, her disappointment apparent. Not being an integral part of Laszlo's extended family made her feel like a fifth wheel, no matter how kind her hosts were.

She took a deep breath, waving to Laszlo and Monica, then gesturing to herself last. "We appreciate everything you're doing. You're wonderful to put us up like this. All of us."

Dori, oblivious to the tension in Erica's words, reached across the table and patted Erica's hand. "Anything for family."

Through the developing conversation, Monica continued gobbling down her meal. Acting as if nothing important was happening, she avoided eye contact with the adults, focusing instead on the warm bread and delicious soup.

* * *

A few clouds drifted slowly across the dark sky, blotting out clusters of bright stars as they moved eastward. A mild breeze rustled through the forest below, and branches swayed under its gentle gusts.

The forest floor was dimly lit, but light from the bright moon provided some visibility in the darkness.

In this dim environment, the Huntsman crouched in a small clearing, moving his covered head to carefully take in his surroundings. He made no sound as he studied the quiet scene, scouring the surrounding woods for signs of life.

But only dark foliage and assorted brush were there to bear witness to his presence in the gloomy meadow.

With a start, the massive man lurched forward, running at a frightening pace through the bushes and low-hanging branches making up the dense forest. With no hesitation in his stride, his legs pumped with blinding speed as he veered through narrow thickets of trees and thick clumps of vegetation.

Practiced and efficient, the Huntsman's movements were controlled and fluid, and no sounds of heavy breathing accompanied his exertions. Instead, he bounded through the dark woods at a dizzying pace, seemingly impervious to fatigue.

Driven yet silent, he bound ahead with an always-forward lean to his frightful stature. His goal, as mysterious as his own strange origin, was fixed on some obscure place far ahead in the darkness. Surging onward, his formidable frame cut an intimidating silhouette against the night.

Climbing a steep hill, he suddenly halted at the top. Peering down, he gazed carefully outward.

Below him, a treed slope descended into an expansive plain filled with orderly vineyards, and occasional lights of lonely houses sat at intervals across the remote region. Around specs of light that evidenced several rural houses, rows of unharvested grapes extended into the distance, quiet and dark beneath the faint moonlight.

The Huntsman stared over the vast area, momentarily still, as if seeking his next destination. Fixed on a point not yet visible, he was looking for a place that silently called to his malevolent mind.

Suddenly, he leapt and grabbed a thick branch. Pulling himself upward, he quickly scaled the tall tree, moving to its highest point with ease.

Once at the summit, he gazed out over the flat ground below the hilltop, peering far into the shadowy night. Across the valley floor, distant lights from varied homesteads glimmered from within the folds of slight rolling fields. The Huntsman's silhouette, perched within the tree's outlines, watched those far-off pinpricks, staying still and meditative while the tree swayed under his weight.

As if his questions were now answered, the Huntsman abruptly lowered himself from the branches. Dropping down, he hesitated, then refocused on the distant lights of Hungary's broad central plain. Tilting his head, he fixated on a specific distant target.

Resuming his controlled rush, the Huntsman plunged rapidly down the hill. Sprinting at what seemed an almost suicidal pace, he raced toward the remote signs of civilization scattered across the vast wine-growing region.

* * *

Nighttime was pleasant behind the farmhouse. A substantial campfire burned in the backyard, casting a luminescent glow across rows of trees that extended into the orchards.

Away from the trees, the cozy house near the circle of flames was itself lit by faint bulbs inside double-paned windows.

Jozsef crouched on a stump in the firelight, peering into the darkness at the fruit trees. He wore a dreamy expression, and a Sherlock-Holmes pipe jutted from his mouth. Tobacco smoke floated upward as he puffed with quiet contentment.

Across the fire sat Erica, Laszlo, and Monica. Perched in lawn chairs, their faces were lit by the crackling flames. Their glowing pupils reflected the fire's light, creating a creepy night-vision-like vibe as they stared across the crackling flames. Despite the situation and surroundings, Laszlo and Erica appeared happy, with their expressions momentarily relaxed.

But Monica was less impressed with the scenery. Scowling, she motioned toward Joszef. "Who uses a pipe? I've only seen that in books. It's stinky."

Erica, growing perturbed, admonished Monica with a stern glare. "Monica, be respectful. I've raised you better than that."

Laszlo and Jozsef both chuckled. Not offended, Jozsef took another drag from the pipe's weathered stem. "That's okay. I've been trying to quit for years. My wife finally chased me from the house, but I sometimes get to sneak a puff or two out here."

Jozsef lowered his voice and leaned toward Monica, as if sharing a secret. "Don't tell Dori about my pipe, and I'll let you drive the tractor tomorrow. Agreed?"

Frowning, Monica considered the offer. It sounded fun, but like all young people, she was torn between tattling on Jozsef and having a good time. Realizing fun was the better option, she nodded.

Leaning closer, Jozsef fist-bumped Monica to seal the agreement. In the background, Laszlo continued his bemused chuckle, smiling widely at both Jozsef and his daughter.

A smile also crossed Erica's face. Momentarily amused, she appreciated her family, and for a few seconds she felt at ease.

After some time, the moment faded. Glancing between Monica and Laszlo, a shadow of sadness pulled at the corners of her mouth.

"Laszlo, shall we take a walk?" Erica suddenly asked, her voice louder than she intended.

Standing, Erica motioned toward the dark rows of trees behind her, a fake smile on her face.

Surprised, Laszlo rose without complaint. Dusting off his hands, he sauntered toward the trees.

"Dear, be a good girl while we're gone," Erica said, smiling at Monica. "Your dad and I are going for a walk. We'll be back in a few minutes."

Walking carefully into the darkness, Laszlo glanced over his shoulder. Worried, he assumed the sad appearance of a dog being taken to the veterinarian, unsure if it would be his last ride.

Monica watched them move away, scrunching her face in confusion at the sudden departure. Resuming her stare at the flickering flames, she stayed silent.

Putting distance between herself and her daughter, Erica moved behind a large apricot tree. Waiting for Laszlo to catch up, she faced her ex. Her expression, even shrouded in the night's deficient light, was irritated. "Well, what's the plan?"

Unfazed and clueless, Laszlo appeared flummoxed. "The plan is, we stay here until they kill that mother—"

"Not that plan," Erica interrupted. "How do we keep Monica from thinking we're a family again?"

Laszlo dropped his gaze, growing silent. His sad features were obvious, even in the shadows.

Growing more annoyed, Monica reached out and touched his shoulder. "Laszlo?"

"What...if I want her to think that?" he asked, hopeful. "Isn't that a possibility?"

Exasperated, Erica raised her eyebrows. "What the hell are you saying? Have you lost your mind?"

"Maybe...we can try again?" he responded, ignoring her question. "To be a couple?"

Erica scoffed, turning away and running her hands through her hair. Disbelief flooded into her voice. "What planet are you on, Laszlo?"

Laszlo glanced back toward the fire, worried about being overheard. He motioned with his hand for Erica to lower her voice.

But she continued, her tone rising. "Who lived in Budapest for two years, getting drunk every night while I tried to give Monica a normal home?"

"Erica, I'm trying to—"

"And who went out carousing every night? Who fucked every cheap whore he could get his hands on, while I stayed home, trying to give our family a good life? To be a good companion to you?"

Breathing deep, Laszlo dropped his gaze. No answer came.

"That's right. It was you, Laszlo. You ruined my life, destroyed my trust. Made my daughter grow up in a single-parent household. All because of you and your fucked-up ideas about enjoying life. It was all fucking you."

Trying to calm herself, Erica took in several tight breaths.

"It was all you," she repeated, her piercing eyes pursuing his, even as he avoided her stare. "And I got nothing for it—except heartbreak."

Raising his sad eyes, Laszlo finally met her gaze. With tears threatening to escape, his pathetic expression was wounded and childlike.

"I know that inside, you're a good person, Laszlo," Erica finally added, allowing herself to sound less harsh.

"I made a mistake, I know it," responded Laszlo, sorrow filling his features.

Surprised, Erica's voice rose again, her rage returning. "A mistake? Let me explain this to you in a way even an idiot can understand. When you're driving, a mistake is when you cut someone off—or maybe bump into them in traffic."

Laszlo blinked, dejected. He still didn't get it.

"It's not a mistake if your car plows through a café, killing twenty innocent people," Erica explained, eyes wide in fury. "That's a bridge too far. Way over the line, to a place you can never return from. Do you get it? Have I made it through your thick, selfish skull?"

"So, you can't forgive me?" Laszlo asked, swimming in self-pity.

Calming herself, Erica lowered her eyes and gave a sad grin. "Laszlo, in the sense that I no longer want you to die a painful death, I've forgiven you. But...I'm never going back into that café, no matter how many bullshit apologies you give me."

Collecting herself, she stepped closer. Her voice was flat and clear, leaving no doubt about her feelings or intentions. "So don't make me the bad person in front of Monica by playing Mr. Family Guy, or I'll never talk to you again. And I sure as hell won't make it easy for you to see our daughter. I've never held you to the terms of our child custody agreement."

Laszlo's sadness deepened into despair. Clenching his jaw, his watery eyes locked on Erica. Something like longing made him quiver, forcing him to stay silent.

Despite his ocean of relationship crimes, his feelings were unchanged, and they were perhaps even sharper than at any other point in their long and shared past.

Without another word, Erica turned and walked back toward the house. Passing the fire, she nodded at Monica and Jozsef.

In response, they stayed silent, avoiding her combative gaze as she stormed past.

With the clack of the door, Erica entered the house.

With the area suddenly quiet, Monica turned toward the orchard and the dark figure of her father, still shrouded behind several limbs. Laszlo hadn't moved from his spot, and he stood carefully in the vague light, staring down at his hands and flexing them in silent frustration.

Monica scowled, her features growing angrier with each passing moment.

* * *

The kitchenette was relatively clean, with rows of plates and coffee cups in an open white cabinet. A shining metal sink lay below, with a rag and a dish-soap container next to the faucet. A wooden countertop ran along the wall, leading to a tall refrigerator that hummed in the otherwise quiet space.

Whistling to himself, Patrik opened the fridge and took out a liter of milk. Moving to the counter, he splashed a generous serving into a steaming cup of water that read "I'd die or kill for COFFEE."

Setting the carton aside, Patrik pulled out a glass container of sugar and ladled six large spoonfuls into the bubbling hot liquid. He worked carefully, focusing on the task like a brain surgeon examining a particularly difficult surgical case.

Mixing the sugar with two scoops of instant coffee, Patrik nodded, satisfied with the perfect equilibrium of brain-starting caffeine and diabetic sweetness. Pushing his glasses up his nose, he sauntered from the kitchenette into a large, sparsely lit research library.

Moving gingerly past several rows of desks, Patrik balanced his steaming cup as he glanced at cluttered bookshelves lining the walls. Only a few lights illuminated the space, making the otherwise comfortable work areas near the shelves feel lonely. Darkness peeked through several dingy curtain-covered windows on the building's exterior wall.

The library was empty except for Patrik. He stood for a minute, surveying the area with a smile as he sipped his cup.

Sighing, he realized that nobody ever claimed the life of an academic was exciting, but the truth was this quiet and closed-off existence suited him. People had a way of being annoying, whether they intended to or not, and he generally preferred to avoid them. In Patrik's mind, it wasn't personal, it was just part of enjoying life as best he could.

Frowning, he moved to a corner table, which was stacked with old manuscripts and books. Lowering himself into the padded chair, he winced, feeling a sharp pain in his gouty leg.

While other men got chronic pain from war or sports injuries, his was a result of sitting on his ass for absurdly long periods. Grimacing, he supposed he could buy a treadmill to rectify his lack of exercise, but that didn't really appeal to his sensibilities. Instead, his commitment to combing through endless archives left him unmotivated to pursue exercise.

Holding that thought, Patrik chuckled. Shaking his head, he knew he was kidding himself. The real reason he avoided exercise was simple: He disliked exertion. Nothing in the world was more reprehensible than sweating and leaning over some loathsome piece of gym equipment.

Inhaling deeply, he reminded himself that next year would be the perfect time to start on the road to physical improvement. He could finally make the effort to address his physical weakness and poor cardiovascular training, making himself into the man he always wanted to be.

That, or he could follow his father's route and go to the grave at seventy without a smidgen of exercise. He had seen his dear father pass away in overweight bliss, frittering away his last years in his favorite chair while watching endless crime programs on his Soviet-era television.

In deep contemplation, he shrugged at that idea, wondering if laziness was perhaps the better option. In exchange for doing what he liked, perhaps seventy seemed like a decent run, full of bagels and unrestrained love of chocolate. *Many healthy people croak much younger than that, in fact.*

Returning to the moment, Patrik glanced around and focused on a set of folders atop a filing cabinet several tables away. Frowning at their messy condition, he stood and trudged over.

Gathering the papers, he parsed through them with a disinterested shuffle of his soft white hands. Endless sheaves of long-forgotten papers, full of useless and obscure information, passed under his eyes each year, so he was accustomed to the boredom they induced.

Shaking his head, Patrik reminded himself to enjoy his efforts. After all, the archives were his life's work, and he knew he might as well enjoy them.

Who else was going to do it? Among his colleagues, he couldn't think of a single person who truly enjoyed this portion of the job. Instead, the others were too busy staring down the blouses of each new generation of fresh students.

Chuckling at that thought, Patrik's grin vanished when something caught his eye. Fumbling, he yanked out some weathered papers from the disused stack of unfamiliar documents. Holding them up to the light, his eyes sharpened as he studied the contents.

Moving to his left, he dropped everything onto the table, spreading the papers out to fully reveal the worn documents. Returning to his chair, he turned on a powerful examination light and moved the bright beam over the papers.

Moving the arm of a magnifying lens, he peered down, his eyes settling on a timeworn page of an official-looking document.

At its top, it read "ANNO DOMINI 1239." Below were several paragraphs in French, as well as scribbled notations in Hungarian that didn't match the orderly writing of the other precise columns.

Patrik squinted, running his finger over the French words and mouthing them silently. As he read further into the account, his expression grew disturbed, like the information was suddenly making him feel ill.

Pressing ahead, he set that parchment aside and carefully examined the next paper.

On this document was a medieval drawing depicting a black-clad man being held against a wall by several soldiers. The man wore a large silver necklace over his dark cloak, and he seemed oddly out of proportion to the other figures in the image. The soldiers pressed the dark figure against a brick wall, controlling him with long polearms of some kind. Their spear-like weapons, six in number, managed to contain the massive man.

A priest stood near the men-at-arms, holding out a crucifix toward the bizarre figure, as if warding away an evil being. Remarkably, despite the crude artistry, the drawing conveyed the vivid chaos of the moment, despite its limited artistic flourish.

For some time, Patrik read through the accompanying text below the scene. His features grew more concerned, with each ancient word forcing a new level of discomfort onto his jowly face. Slowly, his mouth fell open in horrified awe, and he licked his lips nervously.

When he was finally finished, he leaned back from the table. Removing his glasses, he rubbed his eyes, pushing away fatigue with a disquieted scowl. The quiet research library around him suddenly felt very uncomfortable.

Patrik's gaze swept the room, taking in every shadow and prospective hiding place with a twinge of worry. His eyes lingered on each cubbyhole for several minutes, as if expecting someone or something to pay him a visit from their depths.

For once in his life, Patrik felt fear—the fear of the unknown and of things that might really go bump in the night.

It was an odd sensation for a man who had only ever known and lived by science and skepticism. And for the first time in his humdrum career, Patrik wished he had taken up sports instead of boring research.

Chapter Eleven

The morning was overcast, and only a few tourists wandered the streets of the Castle District. The drizzly area was mostly occupied by residents taking morning walks or heading to work, while others stopped for coffee or breakfast as they prepared for their workdays.

Among the few tourist groups, several families gathered at a metal statue of Saint Stephen, the first king of Hungary. The monument depicted a man posed on horseback, staring over the expansive city below and holding a scepter in hand. The statue sat in grand fashion, appearing almost serene as it overlooked its ancient domain.

Near the prominent figure, teenagers from roaming families played grab-ass and shouted in varied languages, while their parents cast disapproving scowls. The embarrassed adults struggled to corral the youngsters into a semblance of order around the important imperial landmark.

The other side of the Danube was just visible at the edge of the morning mist, and a distant horn blared from a drifting barge. The sound and fog somehow created a seafaring vibe, despite the surroundings being far from the ocean.

As if to accentuate the oceanic mood, several circling birds screeched above the water, their calls reminiscent of seagulls in the hazy background.

Across the square, Nemeth paced toward the crowd, a gloomy and determined expression on his face. He still looked weary and short of sleep, but his eyes were brighter in the morning light.

Watching the sparse crowds with a grumpy expression, he searched expectantly for Sergeant Kovacs.

As families parted from Nemeth's hurried path, Kovacs became visible, waving from the base of the tall monument.

Stepping closer, Nemeth noted that Kovacs was gnawing on a pastry and grinning at him. Holding a manila folder, the sergeant was dressed in his formal police uniform, looking decidedly out of place in the touristic environment.

Coming near, Nemeth frowned at Kovacs' breakfast, much of which remained as crumbs still scattered on his uniform. Shrugging, Kovacs offered an uncaring smile and brushed away the remnants of the morning meal.

"Did you get any sleep, Detective?" Kovacs asked, flashing an insincere smile.

"Yes, I did," Nemeth replied, allowing a small grin to cross his lips. "I slept like the dead."

Kovacs chuckled, stuffing the last of the Danish into his mouth.

"That's good," said Kovacs, and he motioned outward, gesturing over the city. "There was nothing new with the killer last night. No sightings, no violence."

Nemeth resumed his severe look, letting his gaze sweep over thousands of uneven buildings below their elevated position.

"That's good at least. He must have gone to ground," responded Nemeth, trying to sound confident but looking unsure. "He knows we'll get him in the long run."

Kovacs held up his folder, tilting his head as if undecided. "Maybe. And...we got back that report from the lab about that liquid from where the killer was shot."

"Good. The results from under the bridge *and* at the baths?"

Flipping through the folder, Kovacs held up two papers and nodded. "Yeah, both."

Impatient, Nemeth opened his eyes wide, letting his eyes bulge in expectation. "Do you need a drum roll to announce it? What does it say?"

Frowning at Nemeth's grouchiness, Kovacs squinted down as he carefully read the reports.

"It says, 'the substance is human blood and is consistent with an ancient sample,'" Kovacs replied, raising his eyebrows. "Says it on both tests with the same wording."

"What the hell does that mean? How's that possible?" Nemeth asked, irritation creeping into his voice.

"Don't know. Maybe it's a mistake?"

"With two different samples?"

Kovacs shrugged and slipped the papers back into the folder. "I'm not a chemist, Detective. But even if I were, it doesn't make sense."

Nemeth went quiet, mulling over the information. Carefully he ran a hand over his stubble in a reflective gesture.

Off in the distance, Nemeth suddenly noticed a crowd forming around the fountain near the Varga's apartment building. What little foot traffic that existed on the square seemed to be accumulating around the Corvinus Fountain. People in the area appeared animated, and as the crowd gathered, muffled shouts and excited talk drifted from the assembled individuals.

Gesturing toward the forming crowd, Nemeth walked in that direction. Frowning and looking harried, Kovacs followed closely behind.

Talking back over his shoulder, Nemeth continued their conversation. "Sergeant, the only time I've heard of an ancient blood sample staying in liquid form is with that church in Italy."

Doubtful, Kovacs pulled even with Nemeth and gave him a puzzled stare. "Never heard of it."

Stopping, Nemeth pondered the distant memory. The information was stuck at the distant reaches of his thoughts, and he couldn't quite recall the specifics.

Scowling, Nemeth motioned toward the fountain, resuming their walk toward it. "It was Saint Janura...something or other," Nemeth finally said, picking up his pace. "It's supposed to be a vial of blood that has liquefied itself on and off for over a thousand years. Since the 700s, I believe."

Nemeth moved closer to the fountain. Shaking his head, he pushed through the chattering tourists, quietly using his bulk to get closer to the source of the roiling crowd's interest.

Close behind, Kovacs raised his voice to be heard over the noise. "Are you saying that it's a miracle, Detective?"

Glancing back, Nemeth shook his head, unsure of how to answer. Pushing on, he flashed his badge to get through the final throngs of onlookers.

Breaking through the last line of tourists, Nemeth stopped at the edge of the fountain. The enormous concrete structure occupied a wide corner of the cobblestoned square.

The fountain was a renowned monument to the most famous Hungarian king, Mathias Corvinus. His hunting party and courtiers were posed beneath him, and water cascaded all around the sculptures. At the feet of the king, a gap marked where a statue should have stood.

Kovacs' jaw dropped. He pointed at the fountain, open shock on his face. "Detective, where is...?"

Nemeth raised a silencing hand, staring at the bizarre scene. People all around the fountain grew excited, their voices rising in a controlled roar.

Taking out his phone, Nemeth opened his mobile browser. Typing in *Corvinus Fountain*, he awaited the search results.

From the side, Kovacs leaned close to see. Several photos of the area directly in front of them appeared. Nemeth tapped on the largest image and pinched the screen to zoom in.

In the photo, the Huntsman stood below King Mathias Corvinus. Holding a spear and sporting a large beard, the Huntsman's pale face was locked in the surreal world of sculptured stone.

In the fountain in front of them, there was an empty gap where that figure should have been standing. The statue was simply not there.

The Huntsman, in its precise outline in the fountain photo, matched exactly with the CCTV images and multiple descriptions of Budapest's raging killer.

Looking up from the phone, Nemeth's shocked eyes locked with Kovacs'. Neither spoke, as they were for the moment unable to grasp exactly what it meant.

* * *

The clear waters of Lake Tisza rippled across open fields of floating green foliage and submerged trees. Varied peninsulas of water connected through waterlogged brush and clumped lily pads, making the waterway seem secretive and blocked off along its dense perimeter.

Created from a dam across a river of the same name, the body of water was large, with vast stretches of pristine vegetation along its muddy banks. Gentle waves lapped against the pebbled shores of the lake's perimeter, and numerous small islands dotted its open surface.

Flocks of birds fluttered through the sky and played on the calm water, providing a busy backdrop on the sunny day.

Laszlo smiled as he peered out across the water from the front seat of a small powerboat, his eyes taking in the lake's natural beauty from behind dark sunglasses.

Looking down, Laszlo focused on the lake bottom through the translucent water. The depth of the lake was shallow throughout, and dark shapes of darting fish congregated within easy view of the surface. Reaching down, he swished the water with his hand, watching its rivulets move around his fingers.

"Can't you tie a lure?" asked Erica, jerking him from his daydream.

Turning away from the peaceful surface, Laszlo looked to the back of the boat. Erica, Dori, Jozsef, and Monica sat scattered throughout the craft, each looking earnestly at him.

Frowning, Laszlo reached down to the line of his fishing pole. He grimaced as he held up a silver lure, a helpless look on his pitiable face.

"I never fished a day in my life," said Laszlo, gulping as he peered at the sharp barbs of the hooks. "It always seemed so…cruel."

Jozsef snickered, removing his pipe to let himself laugh louder. His eyes were lively and amused.

"I'll remember that the next time we eat goulash, Laszlo," Jozsef said, keeping his tone friendly and his features sympathetic. "I don't think the cow appreciated getting gutted for our gourmet pleasure."

Giggling, Dori reached down and pulled up her fishing rod. She proceeded to tie a large fish-type lure within a few seconds, expertly assuring its proper configuration and tightness with a swift tug of her hand. As she gazed up at the end of her pole, a contented grin crossed her face.

"If we look to our emotions to feed us, we'll be hungry most of the time," said Dori, and with little effort, she hurled the lure far across the water. With remarkable accuracy, it fell with a plunk near a thick lily pad.

Erica chuckled at the profound statement, nodding as she got her own pole ready. Growing eager, she grinned at Dori. "I'm stealing that one for one of my classes. And you're invited as a guest speaker at the university. Maybe you could teach the rest of the professors a thing or two about real life."

Even though the rest of the family was enjoying the moment, mostly at Laszlo's expense, Monica moved her gaze behind the boat. Her expression was grim, like she was dreading the prospect of hanging from the gallows but couldn't find a way to avoid such a morbid destiny.

Erica noticed her foul mood. "Mon, are you okay? Try to have some fun. It's a beautiful day."

Scowling, Monica shook her head, staying quiet.

Taking his cue, Laszlo stood and leaned closer to his daughter. Shifting his weight caused the boat to roll slightly, causing Erica's eyes to bulge in worry that they might capsize.

Finding his balance, Laszlo grinned at his clumsiness. Trying to cheer Monica up, he flashed a mischievous smile. "Sweetie, I'm sorry about this whole situation. I'll make everything up to you when this is all over. I promise we'll have a better life. At least, a more normal life. Also, I promise no more Chinese food—at least for you."

Monica kept her poker face, finding no cause to engage with her dad. With no response, she turned and retrieved her fishing pole from the side of the boat. Focusing on her reel, she continued to avoid Laszlo's cheerful gaze.

* * *

This area of the lake was wide open, with few trees or floating brush populating its surface. The shoreline was rocky, and groups of fishermen sat along the water, their lazy lines awaiting a strike by a wayward fish.

Ahead, frothy whitecaps rose on the surface, creating a bumpy ride for the boat. Jozsef's craft plowed gently across the waves, making its way toward a distant set of docks. Around them, there were no other boats on the lake, ensuring a calm and unobstructed ride.

Above, patches of clouds intermittently blocked the sun, reducing the chances of sunburn or excessive heat. As a result, everyone had removed their hats, and Laszlo no longer wore sunglasses to shield his eyes.

Erica now sat at the front of the boat, letting the wind blow against her face. The pleasant breeze cooled her, and she smiled as she enjoyed some hard-earned leisure time in the relaxing environment.

Behind her, Laszlo tried to catch some of the same cool air, but his wandering gaze continued to return to his ex-wife. His constant glances her way distracted him from enjoying the pleasant surroundings.

Farther back, Dori and Jozsef sat near the controls, both with wide grins.

Smiling, Dori gestured at Laszlo's puppy-dog attraction for Erica, but Jozsef merely nodded at the former couple, acknowledging what might have been with a depressed shrug. Unrequited love, even for a man who so deserved the results of his cheating past, was still sad to watch.

All the way to the rear, Monica peered backward at the boat's wake as the vessel plowed through the water. Scowling, her lack of desire to enjoy herself was palpable, and unfortunately, her attitude wasn't getting better as the day wore on.

Jozsef frowned back at her sour mood, puzzling over what might cheer her up. Continuing her despondent gaze, Monica ignored him as her eyes drifted across the beautiful scenery.

Laszlo finally tore his gaze away from Erica, and Dori caught his attention with a big grin. Trying to lighten the mood, she held up a stringer of fish and raised her voice above the boat's thrumming engine. "You may not like to catch them, but I have a recipe you're going to love."

Squinting under the sun's glare, Laszlo merely smiled at the gesture. With a sigh, he glanced again at Monica but failed to elicit any response.

The boat slowed as it approached the docks. It wasn't a large series of slips, holding only a few open slots between bobbing recreational boats.

Several covered boathouses closer to the bank held larger and more expensive watercraft, while to the right a boat ramp was set back from the open water. The recreational area wasn't busy for the moment, but it offered substantial room to launch and recover crafts of all sizes.

Preparing to disembark, the party began packing their supplies from the day trip.

Stuffing several bags of chips into a gym bag, Erica was interrupted by her phone beeping. She frowned and pulled it from her pocket, seeing six missed calls.

Jozsef smiled up from arranging his tackle box and pointed to her phone. "There isn't usually reception for phones on Lake Tisza. I should have warned you."

Erica shrugged and shook her head, uninterested in spoiling her day with the interruption. "It doesn't matter. I'll call them back on the road."

As the boat pulled into their mooring, Laszlo jumped onto the pitching dock to secure the line. Misjudging the distance, he slipped and fell on his ass, nearly tumbling into the water.

Laszlo sat for a moment, his feet splayed wide as he considered his comical circumstance. Chagrined, he peered back at the others.

Concern flashed across his family's faces, with everyone worried he had hurt himself. Rushing forward, Erica hopped on the dock, helping him up and brushing away slivers that had stuck into his shorts.

But Monica was the exception, and for the first time that day, she laughed because of her father's clumsy fall.

* * *

Laszlo smiled from the driver's seat, concentrating carefully on the road ahead. Trying to appear calm, he glanced over at Erica, hiding his enthusiasm for their time together at the lake.

"We should have done that more often," said Laszlo, continuing his awkward grin. "That was more fun than I've had in…forever."

Erica twisted her face, trying to stifle the urge to be sarcastic. She wasn't successful. "Yeah, that would have been nice. Except, I would replace *more often* with *ever*. It wasn't like that lake didn't exist three years ago, Laszlo."

Laszlo's smile wilted, and he didn't reply. He did nod, though, trying to remain upbeat as they twisted down the winding country road.

In the back seat, Monica's bright, curious eyes indicated a better mood as she stared out the side window. Her dreamy face held a faint smile, as if she were suddenly expecting better outcomes in their near future.

On the road behind them, Dori and Jozsef followed Laszlo, trying to keep pace in their older, slower pickup. Plodding ahead, their vehicle's engine revved, sounding as if it was maxed out, as it ascended a slight incline on the narrow highway.

The pair of vehicles drove slowly through the late afternoon shade, carefully weaving over potholes and broken pavement that cut through the forested region.

Erica's face caught as she remembered her missed calls from earlier. Pulling out her phone, she fiddled with the screen and highlighted the last incoming number.

In his office, Patrik picked up on the first ring. Huddled over a cluttered desk, he spoke in a serious tone, as if he did not expect to enjoy the conversation. "Hello, Erica...it's nice to hear from you again."

"Same to you, Mr...I mean, Patrik," Erica replied. "I hope you have some good news for me? You said you weren't interested in pursuing these events?"

Clutching his phone close, Patrik's face flushed. He ignored her reference to his earlier reluctance to help, and this time, he tried to sound brave. "It looks like things have become very bad in the city. I hope you're okay?"

"For the near future, we've moved out of the city, but we're fine," Erica said, dispensing with pleasantries and getting straight to the point. "I saw that you called me?"

"Ah, yes, Erica. I came across something while doing some peripheral research and thought it best to contact you."

"I'm all ears."

"Yes, well, I was filing some documents," Patrik continued, "and I came across some papers that referenced your 'Order of Vengeance.'"

Interested, Erica glanced at Laszlo, who looked bothered at being left out of the conversation. She considered putting the call on speaker but decided against it when she realized Monica would hear everything.

"Okay, what did it say?" Erica asked, resuming the chat.

Pausing, Patrik shuffled some papers, quickly finding some notes he made from his research.

"The documents are primary sources from the Crusades," said Patrik. "It appears they were the basis for how the Order arranged itself for killing all those poor Ottomans."

Erica stayed quiet, but her eyes sharpened, like she was suddenly trying to see Patrik through the connection.

"It seems the Crusaders had a similar encounter with some crazy wretch, precisely as you are dealing with now," Patrik explained, adjusting his glasses and reading his notes with a worried frown. "They comment extensively on a series of murderous confrontations."

Patrik hesitated, clearly reluctant to continue. Sighing, he pushed past his unease. "The Crusaders were threatened in the same way that Hungarian society would be four hundred years later."

Stopping himself, Patrick breathed carefully, carefully biding his time.

"Are you there, Patrik?"

"Yes...well, they were threatened in the same way, but they had a bit more information. It was said that 'vengeance will come in the form of a friend, or someone that is known.'"

Patrik cleared his throat while shuffling more papers. "It also says, 'who brings revenge will do so unknowingly.'"

"So, this curse, this revenge by some psychotic, at least as indicated from the Middle Ages, will get to us from somebody we know?"

"Well, I'm not sure if it is you specifically," Patrik replied, sounding unsure. "This was the part from the last document. They were the ramblings of a maniac who was soon to be executed."

Erica shook her head, confused. Laszlo stared from the side, his desire to listen to the conversation making each second a torturous wait.

"Listen, it's all nonsense, but I thought you should know," Patrik finally said.

Erica considered his words, painfully aware that neither of them thought this new information was nonsense. Unfortunately, it was also true that neither understood the specific importance of it either.

Erica nodded, appreciating Patrik's efforts. "Thanks for the information, Patrik. I don't know what it means, but we are thankful for your time and work."

"It was my pleasure. I'll email you the scans of the documents and my translations, just for your information."

Hanging up, Erica lowered the phone. A dispirited frown crossed her features, mixed with apprehension and dread.

Monica poked her head up front, and both she and Laszlo peered over, showing Erica puzzled looks.

"That...was weird," Erica said, running her palms over her eyes and ignoring their confused expressions. Overwhelmed, she got the feeling something was very wrong in their world. She just hoped someone could eventually explain what it all meant.

* * *

Baffled, Laszlo frowned at the road ahead. They drove on flat ground, with gentle hills and open fields to either side of the deserted roadway. The descending sun had colored the periodic crops and orchards a darker shade of orange in the late afternoon.

"It doesn't help clear anything up," Laszlo said, glancing over to Erica and Monica, as if hoping either of them understood it better than he did.

Getting no response, he shook his head, accepting his ignorance. "Don't worry about it. Solving crimes about crazy people from eight hundred years ago really isn't your responsibility, right? We'll be back at Jozsef's in a while."

Tightening his grip on the steering wheel, Laszlo flexed and drummed his fingertips, growing calmer about their circumstances. "Hopefully, we can figure it out there."

Erica didn't respond, choosing to let her mind concentrate on some as-yet-unknown solution. Concerned, she worried over their uncertain future in silence, hoping that the core danger to their lives wasn't increasing. Being out in a rural area like this, with their secret location tightly guarded, meant they could relax. *Hopefully.*

As the car veered around the next bend in the road, the entire family stared at their worst fear. The Huntsman stood to the side of the paved highway.

In the light of day, the tall and wretched figure was a bizarre sight. He held a vicious black spear at a relaxed angle, its point almost touching the ground. His gray skin, visible on his muscled arms, appeared striated with purplish veins. The spidery effect on his horrid body surface was revolting and entirely unnatural.

His bearded face was still covered by a hood, but there was no mistaking the hulking figure for a normal man now.

The Huntsman didn't move to stop them as they drove by. Confused, he tilted his head, following the vehicle with something like curiosity as it drove past.

Behind Laszlo, the squeal of Jozsef's tires indicated he had also seen the Huntsman. Whatever this figure was, there were now more witnesses to the existence of such a monster.

Accelerating, Jozsef's pickup lurched forward, pushing Laszlo to drive faster as he tailgated with his ponderous truck. Surging down the road, both Laszlo and his uncle increased their speed, frantically putting distance between the now-hysterical family and their odious pursuer.

For several miles, they wound through a series of turns. Eventually, a break in tree cover on the left exposed a familiar rural route, and screeching their tires, the vehicles swerved onto Jozsef's private dirt road.

Chapter Twelve

Laszlo tore down the long road, dust billowing behind his vehicle. Behind, Jozsef also drove too fast, his truck barely keeping traction on the narrow drive.

Terrified, Monica glanced back, then shouted into her father's ear, "Go faster, Dad."

Nodding, Laszlo pressed the gas pedal. The car, not built for off-road driving, plowed ahead, barely staying on the extended gravel-strewn driveway.

Erica looked into the side mirror but could see nothing past the cloud of dust behind them. Frantic, she shouted, "What the fuck was that thing?"

Nobody answered. Blinking, Laszlo was overwhelmed, his mind stuck in looping shock as they sped toward the front of Jozsef's farmhouse.

Slamming on the brakes, Laszlo almost crashed through the pedestrian gate in front of the house. His car slid to an abrupt stop, fishtailing and throwing up a spray of gravel only inches from the property's wooden fence.

Hopping out, Laszlo motioned frantically toward the house.

"Get inside, and grab the rhino gun and bullets," He shouted. Pointing up the road, he waved his hand at Jozsef's incoming truck, which spouted dust as it swerved toward them. "We've got to lock ourselves in until we get some help."

Erica stared in surprise as she processed Laszlo's sudden bent to take command of the situation. Nodding, she snatched Monica's hand and rushed through the gate to the front door.

In the driveway, Laszlo ran to Jozsef's vehicle as it slid to a stop. Impatiently, he banged the rusted bumper with his hand, then leaned toward his uncle's open window.

Peering out, Jozsef met his gaze and blinked several times. Both his and Dori's eyes were wide with fear, and they appeared like lost children in an alien world.

Gathering himself, Jozsef threw the truck's gear into park. Looking harried, he threw the door open and shouted, "What the hell was that thing?"

Shaking his head, Laszlo scanned the road behind them, where a breeze was now blowing away the vehicles' dust cloud. There was no sign of the monster.

"I'm not sure. Get inside and go upstairs. Get any weapons you have and barricade the staircase. I'll hold it on the ground floor," said Laszlo, and meeting Jozsef's stare with a terrified look, he fought back the hysteria clawing at his brain. "But I think it's from hell itself."

* * *

Near the front entryway, Laszlo slung a chair into the growing pile of items blocking the door. A footstool, a small cabinet, and a coffee table lay in a chaotic heap of items meant to slow entry into the house.

For good measure, Monica rushed up, throwing pillows and light kitchen items into the jumbled stack, helping in any way she could.

Above and behind Laszlo, sounds from upstairs were the same. Dori and Jozsef were stacking whatever they could find onto the stairwell, trying to create another barrier against their impending enemy. The pace was slower, but furniture and personal items clattered as they were dropped down and collected on the steps.

As Laszlo heaved a set of golf clubs into the barricade, Erica emerged from a back room on the first floor. Carefully, she laid the large rifle on the kitchen table, followed by a box of ammunition.

"Load it," she yelled. "I'm calling Nemeth."

Yanking out her phone, Erica tapped the screen with trembling fingers. She pressed the speakerphone function as she made the call, her eyes darting toward the front door as she anxiously waited.

In his office, Nemeth sat at his desk. He answered immediately, his face earnest and worried. "Mrs. Varga? I've been trying—"

Erica shouted into the phone, her eyes bulging, "Nemeth, we're under attack. It's a fucking monster. Literally, it's this huge—"

"I know. We've been trying to find you," said Nemeth, keeping his voice calm despite the intense situation. "Tell me where you're at, and I'll have help there soon. We have a helicopter in the area."

Quickly nodding, Erica tried controlling herself, typing furiously on the mobile phone. It took only moments to finish her manic tapping. "I'm sending you the GPS coordinates right now. Hurry."

Nemeth read his screen, then scribbled the numbers on a pad. Snapping his fingers at Kovacs, he threw the pad in front of the sober sergeant, who stood intently behind his own desk.

Holding his own phone to his ear, Kovacs nodded and began relaying the coordinates, speaking in a careful tone.

Breathing carefully, Nemeth maintained his composure, trying to reassure the Vargas as their preparations continued over the speaker.

"Alright, we have your location," said Nemeth. "They'll be there as soon as possible, within only a few minutes. This time they'll be ready—with the right guns, military-grade weapons."

Nodding, Erica hung up and dropped the phone onto the counter. Facing Laszlo, she met his eyes as he closed the breach on the double-barreled rifle with a *chunk*.

Stepping near the stairway, Laszlo yelled up to Jozsef, "Can you see out any of the windows up there? Is he coming? We just have to hold him off until they get here."

Jozsef heaved a bowling-ball bag onto the stairway's middle, where it landed with a thud. Breathing hard from his efforts, he called down sarcastically, "Yes, Laszlo, I saw it coming...and decided to keep it from you. Joking about such matters...is my favorite pastime."

Stopping, Laszlo took the time to grin at his uncle's gallows humor. The crusty old bastard was always cynical, but fortunately, he was also solid and unafraid.

Straightening himself, Laszlo stepped boldly in front of the barricaded front door. Pulling Monica and Erica behind him, he gulped, preparing himself for whatever was to come. Grasping the rifle with white-knuckled fingers, he aimed carefully at the door. And waited.

As the disjointed family awaited the Huntsman, they shook under the stress of the anxious moment. But despite unnerving fear, they stood as one.

Trying to control his breathing, Laszlo spoke quietly, "Maybe the army will get here in time—"

A crash from upstairs interrupted his hopeful words.

* * *

The Huntsman crashed through the skylight, landing among broken glass with little effort. Upright and unhurried, he held his black spear with a firm grip. Panning his head, he searched the extensive second floor living room, ready to thrust at any perceived threat.

The killer's head was now uncovered, and for the moment, he stood perfectly still. Items were strewn around the tile floor and thrown on the stairway leading below. Appearing almost cautious, the Huntsman waited for a response to his raucous intrusion.

Behind him, looking through a crack in a closed closet, Dori and Jozsef stared out at the unnatural thing. They breathed quietly, hoping to avoid its attention.

It was a frightful being to view, this aggressive abomination. The Huntsman's flesh was gray, and its muscles rippled under its strange firm skin. His clothes were draped over his frame in a medieval fashion, with his hood now pushed back to reveal a frightening, wicked face.

The face was encompassed by a huge white beard. His nose was distinctive, giving his features an allusion to an ancient statue-like Greek god.

But the eyes were what made him truly intimidating and evil: There was simply nothing there—no pupil or structure of any kind. The image of this thing was frightening, but the eyes, empty of anything that could be called a soul, made him even worse.

As if sensing them, it turned its eyeless gaze toward the closet. With two steps, it kicked out. The door, shattered and cracked, crashed off its hinges, and the Huntsman cast it aside with a quick swipe.

Stepping closer, the monster leaned down, peering at the rigid couple. Slowly, it raised its deadly spear, ready to finish off the cowering pair.

From below, breaking the dread of the impending execution, Erica's boasting voice called up the stairway.

"We're down here, you stupid fuck."

* * *

At the bottom of the stairs, Laszlo peered up through the barricade of varied household items. On his knee, he aimed the rifle up the stairway. With worried eyes, he motioned for Erica to continue her provocations.

"We're down here, you evil bastard," Erica shouted, raising her tone even higher. "We're waiiiiitiiiing. Come and get us."

Peeking through the remnants of several chairs above him, Laszlo saw a dark leg move onto the stairs. The limb, thick and powerful, took a careful step downward.

Laszlo squeezed the trigger, and a massive *boom* followed. In the narrow staircase, the clap of the weapon's discharge was deafening.

The rifle's kick jolted Laszlo far more than he anticipated, and he dropped backward, falling on his ass and dropping the ungainly weapon. The gun, having been created to dispense death on the open savannas of Africa, was difficult to wield in the confined stairway.

To his side, Erica and Monica cowered from the blast. Stunned, they covered their ears and also fell back.

Above him, the Huntsman buckled, his lower leg blown off by the bullet. Black blood, looking like thick oil, sprayed against the staircase wall, speckled across the wooden paneling.

Recovering quickly, the beast balanced itself with his spear and leapt down the stairs, launching from his good leg.

Laszlo saw him coming and threw himself to the side. Struggling to get his balance, he sprawled and crashed against the wall leading to the kitchen.

Landing with unnerving dexterity, the Huntsman tumbled across the floor, its spear buried in the carpet where Laszlo had just been.

The vicious attacker pivoted on the ground and lunged at Laszlo. With no lower right leg, he pulled himself along with one hand, while the other now clutched a long black knife.

Laszlo frantically tried to put himself between the stone-like creature and his family. Grabbing a chair, he thrust it toward the hulking assailant.

Lashing out, the Huntsman easily smashed the furniture from his hands, sending wooden slivers spraying across the tiled floor.

Scared, Laszlo crouched and took a step back. Pointing to the living room, he gestured madly to Erica. "Go that way. I'll lead it to the kitchen."

As Laszlo leaned toward the kitchen, the Huntsman focused on him completely. Dashing the other way, Erica and Monica rushed to the apparent safety of the living room.

Straining, Laszlo lunged away from his attacker, but the Huntsman pitched forward, tripping him up with a powerful shove.

Falling to his knees, Laszlo sprawled onto the white-and-gray linoleum of the kitchen floor. Struggling, he pulled himself along, trying to get free, heaving himself onward to reach the next room. With panicked eyes and a desperate expression, he fought to get free.

Behind, the Huntsman pawed at him, trying to grab his wobbling legs.

Laszlo kicked at the gray hands, pushing and scraping the floor for traction, trying to create distance to escape the raging predator.

Surging, the Huntsman swiped forward, driving his razor-sharp dagger into Laszlo's back with a wet *thud*. Laszlo screamed in agony, his eyes wide and terrified.

Gyrating, Laszlo tried to pull free from the black blade, but it was stuck fast between his ribs. Bellowing in hideous pain, Laszlo's anguished face was laced with terror.

Crawling closer, the Huntsman sawed further into Laszlo's insides. Piercing deep into his guts, the blade sawed into flesh and organs.

Running into the room, Monica saw the horrible attack. "Daddy. You're hurting him!"

Monica tried punching the horrid assailant, slapping at the Huntsman's huge frame. Crying and screaming, she vainly tried to get the attacker off her dad.

The Huntsman pivoted its head, looking back at Monica and suddenly letting go of the blade. Her ineffectual punches did him no damage, but the monster had stopped its attack.

The unnatural being stood silent as it pulled itself up, balancing on its one remaining leg. It towered over the young girl, swaying and silent. Its gray complexion and empty expression focused entirely on the distraught child.

Monica's sobs mixed with Laszlo's cries of pain.

Moving behind the predatory assailant, Erica thrust the barrel of the huge rifle to the base of the Huntsman's dark skull.

When she pulled the trigger, the enormous BOOM of the shot echoed through the room. With brutal finality, the beast's foul head was cleanly blown from its horrific body. Dark liquid and gray matter sprayed across the room, showering the area in chunky gore.

The killer's body froze for a moment, then quickly collapsed to the ground, as if it were an electric marionette suddenly detached from its power source.

Completely still, the body now assumed the substance of pure stone, but black viscous blood continued to seep onto the slick floor from its open neck.

"Laszlo!" Erica screamed, running to her crumpled ex-husband.

Laszlo lay stretched on his stomach, futilely trying to reach the blade protruding from his back. His legs and free arm kicked and spasmed with pain as he struggled.

Erica stumbled toward him, slipping on the blood-covered floor but catching herself. Crouching, she firmly placed her hand on the knife still embedded between his ribs. Her fingers straddled the blade, trying to staunch the flow of blood.

But it gushed impossibly fast, soaking her hand and coating the ground with shocking speed.

Monica joined her, moving to Laszlo's head and gently cradling his frightened face. With each flinch from the pain, the floor around filled with his pooling blood.

"It's going to be okay, Laszlo, you hang in there," said Erica, tears flowing from her frenzied eyes. "You have a *family* to live for."

Monica's cries grew frantic, her sobs growing louder. Holding her father's horrified face, she wiped across his features, as if the effort would help ease his agony.

Lying on his side, Laszlo struggled to turn his head, to look up at both his daughter and Erica. Seeing Erica, he focused intently, and with something like admiration, he was entranced, recognizing her as the most beautiful and kind woman in the world.

At last, he was with his wife again. They could be together as a couple, if only for this one last moment. Sprawled under her, his pain dissolved in warmth and emotion. A grin crossed his face, revealing bloody teeth and a regretful stare.

Raising his now-pale fingers, Laszlo was just able to brush Erica's face, wiping away one of her tears with his half-clenched hand. In its place, he left a streak of blood.

"I'm so sorry, Erica," Laszlo whispered, his words just audible. A sudden glow came over his complexion, and his face relaxed as his agony dissipated. "I can see everything so clear now. Please...forgive..."

His eyes became unfocused. He looked up at the ceiling, his gentle smile becoming almost joyous. His tense body went limp.

With a gasp, he breathed his last.

Monica screamed in rage and despair, shaking his body, trying to wake up what couldn't be woken.

"Daddy, nooo, Daddy," Monica yelled, yanking and pulling at his face, pleading for him to come back.

Laszlo's blank eyes stared at nothing. His head moved limply with each tug from his daughter.

Pulling back, Erica sat on the floor and sobbed, overwhelmed by the heartbreaking sight of Monica's catastrophic grief.

From the stairway, Jozsef peeked his head out, followed by Dori. Sitting together on the lowest step, they stared at the Varga family, disbelieving and crushingly sad by what they saw. The room, recently so full of violence and struggle, was now quiet except for the sounds of unrestrained sorrow.

Lowering his head, Jozsef now wept, adding his own grief to the awful scene. Misty-eyed, Dori comforted him with a hand on his back, patting gently as she tried to comprehend what had just happened.

And everyone continued to mourn Laszlo, even as the whooping sounds of helicopter blades descended from outside.

Chapter Thirteen

Early morning sunlight flowed through Erica's apartment windows, filling the front room with a pleasant glow. The space was quiet, offering calm where none had existed for some time.

Erica stood near the kitchen counter, focusing on several documents. She scrawled her signature across several papers, pursing her lips as she read between the designated spaces for her name and date.

Coming to the end of the stack, she gently set the papers aside.

With a dreamy glance, Erica cast her eyes around her home, taking in the cozy surroundings with a sad smile. *This perfect apartment is missing a whole family.*

Sighing, she called out to her daughter, "Mon, are you ready yet? We don't want to be late, right?"

From down the hallway, Monica replied, her voice tinged with irritation at being rushed, "I'll be right there, Mom."

Smiling faintly, Erica moved to the window and looked out over the familiar square below. Seeing a cab waiting on the street corner, she nodded and returned to the kitchen table. Numerous manila folders lay on its surface, and Erica took her time arranging them into a stacked semblance of order.

Looking up at the ceiling, her chin trembled as she thought of Laszlo. It was always tragic and sad how people seemed to recognize the obvious only when it was too late to change the path they had chosen in life. She reflected on the man she had once loved so completely, realizing he was the same man who ultimately gave everything for his family. He had been such a bastard, but when it mattered, he didn't hesitate to do what was right.

Reaching into her pocket, Erica withdrew a necklace. Walking to the corner of the room, she peered inside her dark wood-grained china cabinet.

On a glass shelf inside was a framed photo of her and Laszlo, taken when they were on a vacation in New Orleans long ago. They stood with wide smiles on Bourbon Street, a two-level hotel behind them. Their much younger faces beamed at the camera, as if nothing could ever take away their happiness.

Opening the glass door, Erica reached in and draped the necklace around the photo frame. Laszlo's wedding ring hung from the chain, and she left it to dangle across his boyish smile in the picture.

Raising her gaze, Erica was surprised to see Monica standing quietly in the living room. Her daughter was poised near the couch, her eyes teary and pained.

Erica looked directly at her, keeping her tone gentle and considerate.

"The most important thing in life is to forgive, Mon," she said, and glancing back at the photo in the cabinet, her eyes grew reflective. "Never wait too long to act on it. Sometimes...we all need forgiveness."

Monica nodded at her mom, reaching up to wipe an errant tear from her eye. She smiled with a distant, sorrowful gaze as she struggled through her inner grief.

After a long silence, Monica composed herself. "Thanks for going on the field trip, Mom. I didn't want to go alone."

Erica grinned and gestured out the window. "I wouldn't miss it for the world."

* * *

Monica walked out of the apartment building, her mom following closely behind. A single policeman stood next to the entrance, scrolling through his phone and looking bored.

The street around the lobby was lightly traveled. Nobody from the sparse crowds around them paid any attention as mother and daughter strode across the weathered stones into the open square.

Glancing to the side, Monica and Erica looked at the Corvinus Fountain, the source of all the supernatural chaos in their recent lives.

The fountain was completely encased in a heavy tent, with police tape keeping stray onlookers from wandering too close. Several armed soldiers stood around the area while workers in hazmat suits ducked in and out of the tent flaps.

The astronaut-like workers carried pails of concrete and chemicals between the tent and several specialist lab vehicles parked nearby. The whole scene looked like a blend of a science experiment and a military camp.

Gesturing to their waiting taxi, Erica opened the car door for her daughter. Climbing in, she nodded at the driver and motioned for him to proceed.

As the vehicle pulled away, she exchanged glances with Monica, and both looked anxiously back at the covered fountain.

* * *

Heroes' Square was one of the busiest tourist sites in all of Central Europe. Situated at the end of Andrássy Avenue, one of the capital's most expensive and posh streets, it was an immense and wide-open square filled with boisterous groups of pedestrians.

Guided tours with people of various nationalities moved along its perimeter, taking photos and speaking excitedly.

Arranged throughout the square were a multitude of statues and monuments honoring Hungary's greatest leaders, as well as pillars with chariots and horses in glorious poses. Several large museums, as well as an attractive castle, stood around the perimeter of the open square.

Stepping out of the cab, Erica motioned to a large group of children that milled around the statues. Three teachers accompanied the kids, and Erica made eye contact and nodded a greeting as she approached the assembled youngsters.

The children looked happy to see each other, and Hanna, Monica's close friend, waved from the crowd to get Monica's attention.

Excitedly, Monica pointed at her best friend and turned to her mom. "Mom, I'm going to hang out with the other kids while the tour guide talks. Okay?"

Agreeing with a smile, Erica waved her on. As her daughter hurried to the crowd of her classmates, Erica's mood, rarely optimistic, grew buoyant with the lively interactions across the public space.

Catching herself, Erica considered Monica's recent tragedy, which obviously affected both her and her daughter. She was forever impressed with the ability of children to overcome sorrow as they moved through childhood and adolescence. Though young and inexperienced with life, the fact that she was already moving beyond Laszlo's death was encouraging.

With the pang of a distant memory, she remembered a friend from her childhood. Her name was Carrie, a skinny and morose girl, whose father had died suddenly of a heart attack.

Despite the tragedy, Carrie pretty quickly had moved on and lived a normal life, despite the heartbreaking pain she had endured in her impressionable youth.

With an emotional shrug, Erica supposed that was the way that humanity was built—to overcome what initially seemed insurmountable.

Erica strolled gently across the dark cobblestone surface, shadowing the kids as they proceeded from one statue to another.

Monica's smiling face lit up as she looked at each statue. Meanwhile, the tour guide droned on among the wave of kids and tourists. Monica in turn was having a wonderful time enjoying her school's day trip.

Suddenly, Monica's expression hardened. She glanced at Attila, a boy in her class with a bully-like grin and an obnoxious bearing. The young man was teasing other kids on the field trip, pointing and ridiculing them openly.

Monica's gaze toward Attila turned cold and intense, and her burgeoning anger fixated on the boy, causing Erica to lose her mellow mood. Surprised, Erica's breath caught, and for a moment, she barely recognized her own daughter.

The unfolding childhood drama caused strong memories to flood Erica's mind. Confused, she tried to piece them together.

* * *

While shopping at Arena Plaza, Monica purchased a silver pendant from a used jewelry shop. She placed the pendant around her neck, beaming at the beautiful necklace and smiling proudly at her mom.

The pendant looked similar to the one in Patrik's ancient document, the one showing the Crusaders holding back a vicious attacker who was wearing one just like it. Patrik later emailed Erica a copy of that document.

Soon after buying it, Monica and Erica were accosted by the two homeless people who aggressively begged. Erica gave the panhandlers some money, but Monica became angry because of her mom's generosity.

The homeless were later murdered in a dark alley.

* * *

While walking to school with her mom, Monica told Erica how much she hated math and how she disliked both Andreas and Markita Horvath. Andreas was creepy, and Markita was prudish.

Andreas Horvath was ruthlessly slain on Margaret Island, and his wife drowned while trying to escape the Huntsman.

* * *

Monica was attacked by monkeys at the zoo on her last day of school, and Erica shamed Laszlo because their daughter was without a parent when it happened.

Later, Erica watched the news and discovered that animals had been mutilated at the zoo. In an uproar, police were searching for the perpetrators of the crime.

* * *

Laszlo told Erica that the cop Tibor Papp had pulled them over, and Monica was in the car when it happened. Laszlo said the cop was a "complete dick."

He was the same policeman later murdered under the Chain Bridge.

* * *

Monica told her mom that she didn't want Adam around. She also said that Adam wasn't her father.

Adam was brutally killed in his apartment by the Huntsman.

* * *

Near the campfire at Jozsef's farmhouse, Erica yelled at Laszlo, blaming him for their divorce and insisting they would never be a unified family again. Monica must have overheard the argument.

The next day, the Huntsman stabbed Laszlo to death inside Jozsef's house.

* * *

Erica remembered Patrik's words when she called him after their trip to Lake Tisza, when they were on the way home in Laszlo's car.

Reading from old documents, Patrik said, "Vengeance will come in the form of a friend, or by someone who is known." He also said, "...who brings revenge will do so unknowingly."

* * *

Looking up from her troubling memories, Erica grew distressed. She scanned across the square, searching for Monica.

She spotted her daughter standing alone beneath one of the sculptures, staring up at a commanding statue perched on a large concrete pedestal. Her classmates and teachers had already moved on to the next monument.

"Monica," Erica called out, her face filling with panic.

Monica paid Erica no attention, continuing to hold her unblinking gaze on the imposing sculpture above.

Hurrying, Erica pushed her way through the thick crowd. Tourists moved aside as she made her way toward her daughter, but as Erica got closer, Monica continued ignoring her.

Peering up at the statue of King Mathias Corvinus, the greatest of Hungarian monarchs, Monica held a silver pendant in her hand, absently rubbing the ancient metal between her fingertips. Her face was emotionless and distant, as if her mind had completely disconnected from the present.

The unmoving metal statue stood silently above Monica. It leaned on a long curved sword and stared out over groups of tourists and children in the square. The public space was a lively and family-friendly environment, filled with grinning kids and relaxed parents.

Frozen in place, Monica remained lost in her thoughts. She glared up, her eyes entranced with the ancient statue. Her piercing stare was unwavering and fixed, as if nothing else in the world mattered.

Slowly, a knowing smile formed on Monica's lips.

The End

About the Author

Tim lives in Nevada, where he makes a life enjoying all things horror-related, from films to books, and even the occasional convention. He has three children, three cats, and enjoys providing reading entertainment for the monster- and creature-loving masses.

Also by Timothy Bryan

Chindi
books2read.com/u/mlAJ7Z

Despicable
books2read.com/u/49k0ak

By Their Cold Fingers
books2read.com/u/bPgMKr

Core Ruleset
books2read.com/u/mqXyQ6

Prisoners of a Dark Night
books2read.com/u/mllzqW

Praesidia
books2read.com/u/bQ1Rr6